ALICE'S ILLUSIONS

MAYA BLACK

CONTENTS

CHAPTER
ONE

The school bell rang loudly through the halls and classrooms, signaling lunch break for the students. In a flash, the once silent hallways of the high school building were crowded by students milling their way out of their classes and towards the cafeteria.

Trying to peel away from the crowd of students was Alice; a seventeen-year-old blonde with an athletic skinny frame and gray eyes. Alice was somewhat a reclusive figure at school, seeing as she had absolutely no friends and didn't look like she was intent on brushing up on her social skills either.

With her earphones plugged in and Nirvana blasting into her ears, Alice felt like she was in a world of her own. A world where the hideous bullies who cackled at her throughout the length of the hallway were just voiceless ugly gremlins.

Alice wasn't new to being bullied as she had always been at the receiving end of some distasteful jokes by her classmates. She never let it get to her as she barely cared what anyone thought of her.

"Hey, Loo Loo...you heading over to your five-star loo for lunch?" Brad, a burly teenager who couldn't play any sport except lacrosse, jeered at Alice as she silently walked past him and his group of buddies.

Alice barely gave him the time of day as she couldn't make out his words, but the exaggerated laughs she noticed his friends laughing made her somewhat sick to the pit of her stomach. Arriving at an empty bathroom, Alice sauntered in, choosing her most favorite stall and shutting herself in.

She settled down on the toilet and then began to rummage through her paper bag, picking through her lunch as she softly nodded her head to the raging music blasting through her headphones.

Alice had never been one to fit into the crowd and she wasn't looking to. She preferred to be by her lonesome and spent her lunch breaks eating in the bathroom and taking walks to the high school's special rabbit farm which she absolutely adored.

Alice always made sure to make herself available whenever the rabbit farm needed an extra hand, most times causing her to stay longer at school. A faint smile formed on her face as she munched through her lunch whilst thinking about the rabbits, wishing she could have her own rabbit at home.

She was barely done with her lunch and personal musings when the shrill bell rang aloud through the hallways and classrooms again, signaling the end of the lunch break. Groggily getting herself up from the toilet, Alice tossed the remains of her lunch in the trash and washed her hands.

She let out a soft sigh as she paused for a tentative moment in the middle of the restroom, then threw her arms around an imaginary giant rose which she imagined was hugging her. Due to past experiences, Alice was literally immune to bullying and she also did her best to never think about them. Her headphones blaring Nirvana helped her secure the illusion as she walked out of the bathroom and made a beeline for her next class.

Alice's next class was Art class and just like it was customary with the students, very few paid attention as the lecture went on.

Sitting by her lonesome and staring stoically at the whiteboard, Alice picked up on the conversation some girls behind her were having.

"I heard his brother goes here, but he was homeschooled," one girl chimed into the conversation in a hushed tone.

"Well, I heard his name is Hal and he is an only child," another girl countered.

They were apparently gossiping about some new boy in school.

"Oh, well, he is now anyhow. His little brother died last year from what I heard," the third girl chipped in and the conversation suddenly went ice cold as Alice could feel the sea of eyes that were cast towards her.

Alice knew the reason for the unwanted attention was because she knew a thing or two about losing a sibling. Nevertheless, she stayed as quiet as a mouse and never said a word. Deep down, she just wanted to meet this new guy who shared something with her— a lost sibling.

Once the art class came to an end, Alice hurriedly got up and made her way out of the classroom. She made a beeline down the hallway, finding her way out towards the admin block in the distance. She knew if there was any chance that she could get to see this new guy, it would be at the admin building. Taking brisk strides towards the building, Alice got in and carefully scanned around like she was looking for a familiar face.

Unfortunately, the new intakes she'd spotted were either accompanied by their parents or guardians and didn't look like they were in her class either. For some reason, she just knew none of them was Hal, despite never setting her eyes on him.

Carefully moving over towards a list of fresh intakes pasted on a clipboard in the admin block, Alice's heart skipped a beat as she read Hal's full name at the top and realized he was yet to resume.

"Yes, Hal Wood! He resumes tomorrow," a grown man's voice echoed through an open office and Alice peeped in to see a man and woman finalizing paperwork. She guessed the man and woman she was staring at were Hal's parents and after watching them for a tentative bit, she got bored and slipped out of the building and then headed home.

She plugged in her headphones and was back into her own world with Nirvana blaring into her ears. A half smile formed on Alice's face as she walked home, half satisfied that she was going to see a new face at school the next day.

For some reason, she was just elated about it and couldn't wait to meet this Hal guy. If what the girls were saying about him were true, then he was also a handsome boy. Despite her antisocial personality, Alice really wanted to meet this new guy at school as she had a strong conviction that they would be good friends.

CHAPTER
TWO

"Alright everyone, pick a partner and let's get set up for today's experiment," the chemistry teacher announced to the laboratory full of students clad in their white lab coats.

The excited students instantly began milling around the laboratory; friends picking out their friends to be their partners amidst laughing. Within a few minutes, everyone had paired themselves up except for Alice who was seated at a far corner of the laboratory with a blank expression on her face.

The chemistry teacher noticed this and was about to pair Alice into a group when a tall skinny, brown cropped haired boy walked in and handed him a note. The teacher paused briefly to read the note then announced it to the students. "Okay everyone, settle down. We've got a new student here. Make him feel welcome. Thank you! Go have a seat and pick out a partner!"

The teacher nudged Hal's shoulder and the boy briefly spun around to flash a faint smile at the teacher before casting a glance across the sea of eyes gawking at him. Clutching the strap of his backpack, Hal made his way straight to the back of the lab and set up right beside Alice, choosing her as his partner for the experiment.

Alice's heart literally sank to the pit of her stomach once the new boy settled beside her. Regardless, she tried to play it cool as most of the other girls, already green with envy, cast hateful glances back at Alice like she'd done something wrong. Alice wondered why the special new student would choose to sit with her. Hal's arrival at the school was a pretty big deal since they didn't get many new students in their part of the suburbs.

Glancing up at his face, Alice was partially stunned to see none of the knightly, Prince Charming features she had expected from Hal. Instead, he looked like a typical rough-around-the-edges teenager with deep, sullen hazel gray eyes and accentuated cheekbones and jawline. He was about the same age as Alice, but looked like he'd been through something that caused him to age faster. For some reason, Alice began to feel sorry for him when she recalled hearing the girls talk about how he'd lost his brother.

Hal glanced beside himself to notice Alice staring at him. He flashed her a nervous smile which she mirrored as she realized he was just as nervous and quirky as herself. Alice thought he was sweet.

"Hi, I'm Hal." He stretched his hand towards Alice who reluctantly shook his for a split second before reeling her arm. "I'm Hal and I..uhm..I make Hats," he blurted straight out of the blue at a slightly surprised Alice.

"Oh, nice to meet you Hal..." Alice muttered without introducing herself as she never imagined the new boy to engage her first.

"Yeah. Me too. I made this particular hat myself!" Hal beamed with pride, gesticulating towards a cotton woven, rainbow hat he had on.

Alice was surprised the class was still buzzing about the new guy. He was awkward beyond comprehension... and sitting right next to her... *why were all the girls so worried about dating this quirky guy?* These were the questions racing through Alice's mind as she stole sideways glances at the new guy. The teacher requested the entire class's attention and the laboratory went silent as the experiment began in earnest— Alice and Hal working together like they'd known each other for a while.

Once the chemistry class came to an end, Hal swiftly got up, slung his backpack across his shoulder then playfully tipped the visor of his hat at Alice before making his way out of the laboratory.

Alice couldn't help but stifle a giggle which made her feel warm inside as she couldn't recall the last time anyone had given her this much attention. It was almost like she was invisible to the entire class everyday— unless it was time for them to bully her. But with Hal, it was just something different. Springing up from her stool and grabbing her book bag, Alice started out after Hal and caught up with him in the hallway.

"Hey...Hal..." she called out as she walked up to him.

He glanced beside and flashed another kind smile at her.

"I'm Alice." She paused to stretch her arm out towards him with a soft smile.

Hal looked truly pleased by her introduction and took her hand. "Well, it's nice to finally meet you, Alice," he replied and Alice couldn't help but chortle aloud; attracting the attention of some sour-faced girls huddled beside a locker and staring unabashedly at them. Resuming their walk down the hallway, both Hal and Alice fell into a quiet, comfortable walk to his next class; each lost in their thoughts, but basking in the euphoria of the attention their new friendship was attracting.

"Uhm, this is my next class..." Hal slowed down to announce to Alice as they arrived at the door of a classroom.

Struggling to hide the disappointment on her face, Alice feigned a smile. "Oh. Okay. See you around then, Hal," she replied sweetly then spun around to continue trudging down the hallway in solitude.

"Hey, Alice!" Hal called out from behind, almost startling her.

Alice glanced over her shoulder. "I love Nirvana too," he added with an almost sheepish grin.

Alice blushed red at the cheeks and felt embarrassed, hoping he couldn't notice from the distance between them. She could only crack a smile as she wanted to tell Hal it was her older sister's t-shirt. She also wanted to tell him she knew what it felt like to lose a sibling, but held back as she knew that would just be opening up old wounds in a new relationship. "Thanks. See you at lunch!" Alice beamed a grin at him as she walked away.

True to their promise, Alice and Hal found each other at lunch. For the first time in a very long time, Alice didn't have her lunch in the bathroom as she always had. Instead, as she settled beside Hal on the lunch table, he leaned in to whisper. "Are you really hungry for this shitty food?" Silently swiveling her head in disapproval with a half-smile, Alice agreed with him while half wondering what he was up to. "C'mon, let's go!" Hal sprang up from the bench and pulled Alice's arm behind him.

A sea of hate filled eyes trailed their movements as they exited the cafeteria in a flash, leaving behind the other murmuring students who couldn't explain the connection the new boy had with quirky Alice. Stepping out of the building, Hal and Alice made their way towards the school's football field then found a cozy shaded spot underneath the nose bleed bleachers.

Alice still hadn't said a word yet as she couldn't understand why they had dipped from the cafeteria to come here. But she kept mute, nevertheless, fascinated and equally intrigued by Hal's strangeness.

"This should do..." Hal mused with a smirk as he fished into his backpack, pulled out a pack of rolling papers then half an ounce of crushed weed in a ziplock bag. Alice's eyes flew wide at the sight of the psychedelic plant in Hal's hands as she'd heard much about marijuana but had never tried it out. "Ever had one before?" Hal asked as he began to expertly roll up a joint.

"No...but uhm, my sister...my sister used to indulge sometimes, I think," Alice stuttered a bit as she watched Hal's fingers and tongue work assiduously to create an almost perfect joint which he stuck between his lips then flicked a lighter at the tip. The joint sizzled to life, releasing its aromatic essence into the cramped-up space the pair were huddled at. Hal showed off a bit, puffing clouds of smoke up in the air to make a fuzzy 'O' shape before it dissipated into the wind.

Alice giggled a bit at the trick and Hal handed her the burning joint. Taking a long drag of the weed, Alice could feel her sensory organs moving into a rather calm but edgy overdrive as all her senses were suddenly heightened and her feelings elevated. She puffed out a thick plume of smoke, much to Hal's admiration before handing it back to him after a mild cough or two.

"That's okay. You'll get the hang of it eventually." Hal smiled as he puffed another cloud of smoke then in the most random fashion, he asked her, "Who's your favorite dead celebrity?"

An eerie silence enveloped the pair after Hal's question before Alice replied. "I think Kurt Cobain," she piped up.

"Hmm...can't knock that. Dude had crazy talent. His death sucked," Hal agreed with another puff and pass of the joint.

"How about you? Who's your favorite dead celebrity?" Alice asked with lazy eyes and a stoned grin etched on her face now, as she puffed from the joint.

"Urggghh...let's see..." Hal glanced up with a slight groan like he was in deep thought. "There's quite a few actually..." he trailed off.

"Name them." Alice was totally free with Hal now and wanted to talk about everything with him.

"Well, there's Mac Miller, there's Amy Winehouse...and oh, John Lennon!" he added emphatically.

"Hmmm...quite a list, huh?" Alice hissed softly after a drag of the joint which she then handed back to Hal.

"Tell me about it. The good ones never seem to stay around for long." Hal shrugged then took another long hard puff of his joint.

Alice was silent now, half wondering if Hal made his last statement in reference to the actual dead celebrities or his dead brother.

Alice wanted to bring up the topic of Hal's dead brother and her dead sister, but she felt there was no point in ruining the good moment with such sordid feelings.

"I like your hat. You said that you make them?" Alice randomly asked to change the trajectory of the discussion into a lighter mood.

Tapping on his head like he'd forgotten he had a hat on, Hal smiled at Alice's remark.

"Thanks! Of course, I do," Hal quipped with pride. "Hold on," he said as he reached for his backpack lying on the ground and began rummaging through it, pulling out woven hats of different colors and color combinations so Alice could see.

Alice was a bit stunned at how serious Hal took his hat making but didn't show it. "Wow...these are so cool!" Alice beamed a full smile at Hal as she admired and held up different hats to view them. For some unknown reason, it made her feel warm knowing Hal was enjoying his time with her and she didn't want it to end. They both heard the grueling sound of the school bell shrilling through the compound; signaling the end of lunch break, and groaned before laughing and heading to their next classes.

THREE

Due to her parents always being busy, it was a rare occurrence to see both of Alice's parents home at the same time. They often worked overtime and barely spent time with their kids, at least since Alice's sister had died. But today, however, they'd both decided to come home early to spend time with the kids.

In that effect, Alice's mother had also made a pathetic attempt at a homemade dinner of charred chicken with a horrible salad dressing. Alice could barely touch her dinner, but her brother meandered his way around the charred chicken; digging into the soft innards of the charred poultry and munching away hungrily at the table. Alice barely cared that she wasn't eating anything as she knew her father would get her Panda Express as an apology for her mom's horrible cooking. It was like an unspoken rule of thumb between father and daughter and she didn't need to remind him.

Occasional casual glances at his daughter's untouched plate was enough to point out to her dad to get her Panda Express after the tasteless dinner was done.

"So how's school?" Alice's mom asked to break the monetary silence at the table.

"Fine," Alice casually replied with a hidden eye roll.

"Danny's older sister says you're hanging out with that creepy kid," Alice's younger brother—Ethan, randomly blurted out.

"ETHAN!" Alice angrily reproached her carefree brother with a darting glance.

Alice's parents exchanged quick glances before fixating their eyes on her and asking almost in unison, "What creepy kid?" One could easily tell they were troubled by the news and were more interested in knowing who this kid was, just by seeing Alice's defensive countenance.

"Ugh! He's not creepy!" Alice groaned back, clasping her head in her hands for a moment. She pulled her hands away and scoffed aloud. "Look, he's not creepy in any way, he just likes the type of bands our sister was into before..." Alice slurred off and an eerie silence enveloped the dining table as her sister was a tabooed topic in the house. "What?!" Alice blurted out in swelling anger. "You guys can't just keep acting like she didn't exist!" she snapped at everyone at the table then sprang up, storming off to her room in anger. The awkward silence lingered as everyone else exchanged knowing glances while watching Alice walk away without stopping her.

IN THE SOLITUDE of her room, Alice was a bit sad and let down that her father hadn't followed through with their silent agreement to sneak her and her brother Panda Express to placate her for her mother's horrible cooking.

Laying down on her bed, she rummaged through her book bag and began to finish up her homework. Once she was done, Alice's attention shifted to a big box of clothes which had belonged to her dead sister. Rummaging through the box of clothes, Alice fished out a pair of denim shorts and a metal branded tee shirt which she tried on and admired herself in the mirror afterwards.

A subtle knock on Alice's room door suddenly made her agitated; refueling her anger from earlier and making her scream at the door. "GO AWAY!"

"Alice, honey, it's me. I've got your Panda Express right here," Alice's father's voice echoed through the cracks of the door frame into her room, making her pause for a bit to rethink her decision.

"Come in," she finally said, her stomach making her give in before she really wanted to.

After a tentative silence elapsed, the door slowly opened up and Alice's father snuck his head in before other parts of his body after seeing a sour-faced Alice standing in front of the mirror.

"Hey, hon. Here you go." He flashed a smile as he handed Alice the takeout.

Alice took it from him without saying a word and another awkward silence elapsed between father and daughter.

"Finally..." he sighed with a wry smile to break the silence. "Alice, you really hurt us, you know? It's not that we want to pretend Jane didn't exist, Alice. It's that her memory hurts so much that sometimes it's easier to not talk about her."

He paused to sigh again, almost like the words were too heavy for him to speak but he carried on. "You must hear your mother crying at night, me walking the halls, and your little brother waking up with nightmares. We all remember, Alice. We remember too well." He took another pause and looked straight into Alice's eyes. "I think perhaps you forget that your sister was not a saint. She left some of us with more scars than others."

Alice's blood boiled inside of her with such a rage that she'd never felt before in her life. With the fuming anger inside of her, she tossed the takeout right at her father, soiling his tee shirt with the contents as she screamed. "GO AWAY! How dare you talk about her like that?!" She ran into her bathroom sobbing and slammed the door shut.

Alice's father remained rooted to the spot for a bit before he reached down to pick up what he could from the ruptured takeout and carefully made his way out of his daughter's room.

FOUR

"Woah...that's fucked up!" Hal took a hit of his joint underneath the shade of the bleachers, which had become their favorite go to spot every lunch break. "Why would your dad say such a thing? I mean, what did your sister even do that was so bad?"

He took another hit of his joint and Alice listened to how the rolled up herbs sizzled in the burning paper. It sort of reminded her of how fickle everything called life was.

Wearing a sullen expression on her face and staring off into nothingness, Alice blinked back from her reverie and turned her attention to a red eyed Hal. "I think he is right about one thing. I have forgotten," she started off in faint recollection, her face scrunching up like putting up the pieces of this ripped picture was the hardest thing for her to do. "There are chunks from ... before ... that I can't seem to remember. Moments leading up to her suicide... Maybe he is right. Maybe I forgot that she was a monster." She stared wide eyed at Hal.

"Monster or not, I deserve to grieve," she mused in a soft defensive tone and before she knew it, Hal closed into her and threw his arm around her shoulder and pulled her close, holding her tightly for what seemed like an eternity. Alice could hear the thudding of his heart as she meshed close to him and she also held onto him tightly; savoring the warm feel of his clothed masculine frame.

"I lost my little brother a year ago as well," Hal began to break the momentary silence. "Something my parents still blame me for till this day." He scoffed in almost disbelief at the tough luck life had handed him.

Alice slowly pulled her gaze up to stare at him. She pulled back but stayed close to him so she could lean against his shoulder while he carried on with his narration. For some reason, she just knew it was better to keep quiet and let him finish than offer condolences which wouldn't do shit.

"We were out ice skating like we always do," Hal continued. "I'm always careful. Dad taught me how to be, you know?" He turned to her and she nodded affirmatively like she understood him perfectly, but it never even snowed where she was from. "My bro says he wants to make a video for his YouTube channel. He hands me his phone, does these crazy cool ice skating tricks which totally blew my mind..." he paused to chuckle softly here; a laugh mixed with pain and sadness. "Apparently I didn't see my brother skating far out onto thin ice and one acrobatic flip from him was all it took for him to plunge into freezing water. He was well below twenty feet and still drowning by the time I ran across." Hal let out an exasperated sigh as the school bell rang out; signaling the end of lunch break.

A befuddled Alice could only stare at him in pity as she moved her arm to the nape of his neck and gently caressed him. "It's not your fault," she whispered softly.

Hal turned his attention to her and nodded softly, pulling himself up and grabbing his backpack which oddly followed him everywhere as he never seemed to make use of his personal locker.

"HEY ALICE, isn't that your dead sister's shirt?!" Mary Anne, a heavyset, red faced bully, teased Alice as the latter walked through the school's hallway towards her morning classes. Alice had to fight back the tears welling up in her eyes as she kept strumming down the hallway; eyes down and music blaring in her ears, albeit just loud enough so she could still hear the distasteful things the bullies had to say.

"Yeah Alice, you should let the dead rest," another burly teenage boy cackled at Alice from his locker as he turned to glance at her. "Matter of fact, that shirt looks too big on you. You're gonna have so much growing to do to fit into it. Which is something your sister unfortunately can't do...grow." The group of bullies all erupted in an eerie cacophonous laughter which made Alice hurt deep down as she fought the tears from streaking down her cheeks in rivulets.

"SHUT THE HELL UP, FATSO!" Hal's voice thundered from behind the action as he briskly walked up to the bullies all up in Alice's face.

"Yo, who the hell is the new guy here calling fatso?" The pissed off bully faced Hal. "You want a piece of me, huh?" He confronted Hal and in a flash, Hal grabbed him by the collar of his shirt then slammed him back first into the lockers; a loud bang echoing through the hallway as he held the stunned bully against the lockers.

"New guy here is the one who's gonna bash your pudgy face in if you don't stop talking shit about her dead sister!" Hal sniggered with disdain at the stunned bully.

"Alright...alright man. I was just joking, okay?" The bully could see the ice cold veins popping out of Hal's eyes and he knew better than to piss off the new guy with a shady background history of possibly being responsible for his brother's death.

Angrily letting go of the bully as a sea of eyes had watched the action now, Hal spun around and then grabbed Alice by her arm, whisking her away from the crowd of students in the hallway. Alice had never felt so protected in her life and she wished she could repay

Hal for standing up for her, something no one ever seemed to do for her.

Hal walked Alice to her last class before lunch. "I'll meet you here after class and walk with you to lunch. Then no one will mess with you, the assholes."

"You don't have to do that, I can deal with it."

"Nonsense, I want to do it. I'll protect you. Wait for me."

Alice looked at him and answered as she walked through the door to class, blushing brightly, "Ok, I'll wait for you."

CUSTOMARY TO THEIR NEW TRADITION, Alice and Hal went straight to the bleachers to have their lunch and talk about everything.

"Those fucking assholes!" Alice muttered absentmindedly as she munched on a bagel and chewed slowly on it.

"Hey, let it go. We're definitely gonna make them pay this Halloween. All of them!" Hal rubbed her shoulder almost affectionately, gazing amorously into her eyes with a soul melting smile.

"Oh, I'd sure love that," Alice replied with a beaming grin. "What costumes and props are we gonna need?" she asked eagerly.

"I'll send you a list when we get home," Hal replied.

"Cool. I'll tell my mom to take me shopping for them. Can't wait to see those suckers piss their pants when we get 'em!" She sniggered and Hal chortled softly then reached into his backpack after he was done with his lunch.

Alice watched as he pulled out a different hat from any of the ones he'd shown her before. "You just made this?" Alice asked before he even said anything and she noticed Hal's proud smile at her stellar recognition of his works.

"Yes, I just did. It's pretty cool, huh?" He stretched out his arm holding the hat so she had a good view of it.

"Indeed. It's lovely," Alice commended him with a sweet smile.

"Thanks," Hal replied as he returned the hat to his backpack and zipped it close.

"Have you ever tried communicating with your dead sister?" he asked randomly after a brief pause between them.

Alice was at a loss for words at such a question that she didn't even know how to reply to him. *What did he mean by communicating with her dead sister?* "Uhm..I'm not sure I get what you mean, Hal?"

"Okay, listen here, Alice. It's not rocket science. You actually can connect with your dead sister by a few means which I myself happen to be knowledgeable on," Hal tried explaining to a still confused Alice.

She'd only read and seen this type of stuff in books and movies. It was partially mind boggling that Hal was into it, but also enthralling that she could get the chance to converse with her dear sister and ask her all the questions she had about her suicide.

"Okay...and how do you get to communicate with these spirits?" Alice asked after Hal was done.

"Can you meet me at the park, 9pm tonight?" Hal asked in a serious tone.

"Uhm..sure!" Alice replied.

"Good! I'll show you then!"

CHAPTER
FIVE

Alice was wriggling her arms up into her turtleneck sweatshirt when a familiar knock rapped on her room door. "Alice? It's Ethan," her brother called out from the other side of the door.

Puffing out an exasperated air of frustration as she already knew what her brother's visit to her room was all about, Alice groaned her reply as she eased into her shirt then sat at the edge of her bed. "Come in."

The door creaked open by a crack and her brother slipped in, half surprised to see Alice dressed after not seeing her at dinner. She had been deliberately avoiding everyone at home, especially her parents. She had even gotten herself Panda Express and imagined how visibly displeased her father would look when he found out.

"Hey..." Ethan said as he shut the door gently and leaned against it.

"Hey..." Alice replied coldly, casting sweeping glances all around herself as she searched for the lost pair of her socks.

Ethan wanted to ask her where she was heading off to but chose to save that question for later in order not to infuriate her further.

"You know all's not well between mom and dad since your outburst," Ethan, who was the only one Alice could listen to without getting aggravated, informed her of the state of the family. He let out an exasperated sigh as he walked over to sit beside Alice and watch as she struggled into each sock; her blonde hair bouncing around her face as she moved with a sense of urgency. "They've been fighting so much," Ethan continued. "I miss her too, you know?" He exhaled and stared at his almost nonchalant sister.

Alice finally paused from her movements and turned to face her brother, scooping back her blonde hair behind her ears and forcing a smile on her face as she noticed her brother was pouting.

He really was the happy-go-lucky type who felt miserable the most when their parents fought. The last thing Alice wanted was her brother to feel the ripple effect of their sister's death as she could tell he was also struggling hard to get past the traumatic experience of losing a sister. His nightmares were recurrent and he visibly struggled to cope without his big sister who helped him out with his assignments and usually gave him the slippery slope by taking his homework all to her room and tossing them back on his bed when she was done. Ethan recalled how astounded he used to be when the results came in and he never scored below excellent marks. His sister was a genius but never showed it. Rather, she felt repulsed by the idea of being regarded as 'book smart'.

Gently tugging on her brother's cheek, Alice replied. "I'm sorry if my outburst made you feel bad." She reeled her arm back and sighed. "It's just...she doesn't deserve to be remembered like that, you know?" She glanced at her brother after her rhetoric.

"I agree. Dad was out of line. But we're all dealing with it however we can, I guess." Ethan shrugged coyly, staring at the Nirvana band poster plastered on the adjacent wall of his sister's room. He silently wondered if his sister's recent affection for the genre of music was influenced by their dead sister.

Alice was also in deep reflection, thinking about what her brother had just said. He was right. Everyone had to deal with Jane's loss however they deemed fit. She knew she couldn't tell anyone how and what to feel but she was definitely going to get her answers.

Suddenly snapping away from his reverie and breaking the shattering silence that enveloped the room as both siblings were momentarily drowned in their thoughts, Ethan glanced over at his sister from head to toe, acting like he was just realizing she was fully dressed at nine pm. "Don't tell me you're already getting invites to frat parties?" he blurted out and Alice couldn't help but erupt in a soft, hearty laughter which filled her with happiness for a good while. "What? I know for sure you're not heading out the front door by this time. So what's up?" Ethan shrugged his shoulders with raised eyebrows, causing Alice to laugh for a bit longer.

"Okay, first of all, I'd literally be found floating stiff as a board, on a lake, rather than be found at a frat party!" Alice quipped at her brother.

"Uhh...that's gnarly!" Ethan retorted. "Seriously, where are you going?"

Pausing for a bit, Alice's smile wiped off her face. "Ethan, I'll need you to help me keep a secret," she announced softly to capture her brother's rapt attention.

"Okay..." he said in reply.

"I'm going to talk to Jane..." an eerie, awkward silence followed as Ethan kept mute, knowing that definitely wasn't all that was there to be said, "...with MAGIC," Alice whispered emphatically as she leaned towards her brother with expressive brows and eyes.

"Woah...are you sure about this?" Ethan finally asked once he noticed Alice was dead serious.

"Yes, but I can't talk much about it until I'm back so I need you to keep this between us, okay?" she quipped rhetorically with a sense of urgency as she sprang up from the bed after half-struggling into her pair of white sketchers.

"Oh...okay. Sure. You got it. Tell me all about it when you're back," Ethan replied, still in slight disbelief at what he just heard.

"Of course. Now lock the door on your way out then slide the key underneath." Alice winked back at her half-stunned brother as she made her way out of her room window and disappeared into the night.

CHAPTER

SIX

A few minutes of jogging through the near empty streets, Alice could make out the silhouetted image of a rather impatient Hal, pacing around a dry fountain sculpture in the park. "Hey. Sorry I'm a few minutes late. My brother ran into me on my way out and I had to make sure he wouldn't spill," Alice explained as she tapped Hal by the shoulder and watched him pause then turn around.

She noticed he was clutching an Ouija board underneath his arm as he glanced sideways, almost like he was confirming Alice hadn't been followed. "Hey...I said I took care of him. No one followed me here!" Alice picked up on Hal's shifty glances and quickly reassured him they were alone; which was a bit scary for her when she thought about it. She quickly shook any negative thoughts out of her mind as Hal's glassy eyes stared into hers, almost making her go weak in the knees. His eyes had a somewhat imposing and enchanting gleam to them underneath the dim lights of the streetlights that were partially illuminating the park. She'd never seen them glitter in quite this way.

"It's fine. I trust you." Hal smiled warmly at Alice and she felt butterflies flutter all in her stomach as he did that thing where he led the way while grabbing her authoritatively by her arm, albeit gently but persuasively. "C'mon, we don't have all night," Hal quipped as he led them towards a park bench in the far corner of the park, barely illuminated by the lights and shaded by huge trees. Spreading out the Ouija board once they both sat on the bench facing each other, Hal glanced up at Alice with stone cold eyes. "Ready to talk to your sister?"

An eerie chill ran up Alice's spine as she instantly began to contemplate if this was just a stupid idea brought about by her desperation for answers. She wondered if Hal was trying to benefit somehow off her woes but no matter how much she tried to think about a motive, she never found one. This made her, in turn, trust Hal more as he seemed to be the only steady pillar of support in her life right now. Letting out a soft sigh as she scratched her neck while staring at the planchette that looked like it had seen more than a decade, Alice replied, "Are you sure this is gonna work?" Her reluctance was visible on her face.

Hal scoffed as he began moving the important pieces on the board and in a firm tone, he replied, "You don't have to believe. Just ask your sister whatever and watch the movements on the board."

"Oh...ok, you mean right now? Okay," Alice stuttered as she sat up and tightened her hair in a neat ponytail. She wasn't about to miss even a flicker of action on the Ouija board.

"Close your eyes, take a deep breath and call out your sister's name three times," Hal ordered in a firm tone once Alice was done with her hair.

Truly wanting to believe Hal, Alice shut her eyelids tight, took a few deep inhales and exhales before calling out Jane's name three times into the silent night. She felt the chill of a gust of wind sweep past her the third time and when her eyes flew open she just knew something had changed in the atmosphere.

Hal's fixated eyes said the same thing too as he casually glanced around at nothingness then back at Alice. "Your move." He nodded softly at the Ouija board.

Clearing her throat while fighting the eerie chill crawling up her spine, Alice called out. "Jane? You there? I need answers, Jane. A whole lot of things just don't make sense since you've been gone." Alice paused for a bit and was replied by a cold silence for a good minute. She was about to give up and glance away when Hal called her attention to the moving pieces of the board that spelt out the simple word; 'TALK'.

Alice swallowed a hard lump in her dry throat as she stared wide eyed at the board then up at Hal who nodded silently at her to carry on. Feeling more confident about the spiritual endeavor now, Alice's voice grew louder now. "If you're really Jane, then what's my birthday?" Alice called out into the night.

This time the board didn't waste time to reshuffle its pieces; presenting Alice's exact date of birth right before her. Her heart skipped a couple of beats as the hairs at the nape of her neck stood up. It really was Jane. Her heart fluttered with joy and a single tear of happiness ran down her face. Alice swiftly wiped the bead of the tear away and carried on while Hal remained silent. "Why Jane? Why did you leave us? I've been hurting ever since," Alice asked as she stared at the board spell out 'sorry, couldn't take it anymore'.

Alice's heart sank to her stomach as she realized her sister had been battling privately with some really horrible demons that had won eventually. She wanted to know what exactly happened. Still tethering between belief and denial, Alice randomly asked the board, "Can you tell me how you died, Jane?"

Alice's heart literally stopped as she watched the board spell out the words; 'Bathtub, pills overdose, slashed wrist so nobody could save me'. Alice felt an instant gut wrenching sensation in the pit of her stomach at the reply she was staring at. She recalled how she had stumbled on pictures of the suicide scene taken by the cops and had cried her eyes out at how horrific Jane's death had been. She wiped off another approaching tear with the back of her hand while Hal still observed her with almost emotionless eyes of steel.

"Are you okay?" Hal finally asked as Alice had been sobbing for a few minutes now and was unable to carry on with her questioning. Hal could still feel Jane's spirit lingering but knew she wouldn't be around long enough for Alice to get all her answers.

"Yes, I'm fine. I'm fine!" Alice cleared her throat and sniffled as she stopped sobbing. She was already red in the face but still wanted to keep going. She needed more answers. "Why, Jane? Why did you do it? TELL ME WHY!" Alice's voice piped up emphatically and breathlessly, her tone riddled with raw emotion of all the pent up pain she had endured since her sister's demise.

For some reason, Hal held up his arm at this point, swiveling his head in disapproval of Alice's question.

"Don't fucking tell me what to do!" Alice suddenly snapped at Hal with unbridled profanity and fiery gaze in her eyes. She quickly recollected herself, cupped both palms over her face and took one deep breath to ease her mind. "I'm sorry, but that's against the rules, right?" she asked with slumped shoulders.

Before Hal could reply, both their attentions were snatched by the planchette that had resumed moving again to spell out the word, Secret. Alice scrunched her face at the message and before she could say anything further, a flock of loudly cawing ravens flew right past them, causing both teenagers to shield their faces with their arms as Alice clearly felt a few feathers ruffle past her raised elbows.

The flock of ravens dissipated into the dark night just as randomly as they had appeared, causing Alice to take quick breaths to calm her agitated self. She needed to head home. "I'm going home," she announced to Hal as she sprang up from the bench, cupping the stray strands of blonde hair from her face.

"Okay. See you at school then," Hal casually replied as he watched Alice spin around and resume her quotidian brisk walk she did whenever she was nervous.

"No way that was real. No fucking way!" Alice muttered to herself on the way home as she meandered through the dark streets. She still couldn't believe that she had just had a conversation with her dead sister. Alice was visibly shook as she hugged herself in fright while walking fast through the streets; her anxiety and hypomanic state riding high. *Could it really be true? Did that just happen? What was it with those ravens?* These were the slew of thoughts that besieged Alice's wandering mind as she made her way home; nervously glancing behind her shoulder at intervals, not knowing exactly what to expect.

She recalled how Hal had seemed so out of it today. *What was with the pacing before she arrived? Did he consult his dead brother before she arrived?* She had been so engrossed in herself that she had even forgotten to ask Hal if he had ever spoken to his brother through the same medium. Carefully tiptoeing her way around the house, Alice made her way towards her brother's room window, intent on telling him everything that had happened as part of keeping her own end of their bargain. She also wanted to be sure she wasn't crazy and hadn't imagined everything she'd seen tonight. Thankfully, Hal was her witness.

"Are you still up?" Alice whispered into her brother's room as she slid open his window and snuck in.

Turning on the light at his bedside, Ethan squinted up at the figure of his sister at the window. "Oh, you're back from your shaman. How was it?" He groaned softly as he rubbed his eyes.

"It wasn't a shaman, Ethan. It was real. I spoke to Jane!" Alice retorted in a firm tone that made her brother sit straight up with widened eyes.

"Shut the front door! There's no way that happened!" Ethan exclaimed in a hushed tone with a scoff.

Alice hurried over to his bed and sat beside him, staring him right in his eyes. "She told me exactly how it happened. How dad found her and called the cops before we got back from school. She told me everything Ethan," Alice quipped with a shaky tone which she cleared up in order to not break down before her brother.

Ethan seemed equally stunned by the revelation as he was left gobsmacked for a good minute. There was no way Alice would joke over such a sensitive topic as their sister's death. He also began asking her questions.

Alice spent the night serenading Ethan with a blow-by-blow account of her mediation with their dead sister. She told Ethan how Jane still remembered her birthday just as she was always the first to do when she was alive.

Ethan couldn't help but let a tear escape his eye at this point. Jane used to get him the best birthday presents, not minding if she cleared out her savings to make him show her that big mischievous grin of his. "Did she say why she did it?" Ethan finally found the courage to ask Alice after listening to her.

An eerie silence followed as Alice slipped further into Ethan's bed and pulled up the duvet while staring up at the ceiling, almost absent-minded. "No...other than she couldn't take it anymore," Alice replied in a hushed tone, still staring unblinkingly at the ceiling. She also silently wished Hal hadn't interrupted her when she was asking the questions but she knew she wouldn't have done all of this without his help. She wondered if he helped grieving families with mediation or it was just something he did because they were good friends. Whichever way, she knew she was going to be seeking him and that Ouija board again really soon.

Confused as to what that meant, Ethan probed further. "Take what..?" He thought it was strange that Jane would leave Alice with half truths and not the entire story of what had actually happened to her.

"She didn't say, Ethan." Alice could feel her eyelids growing heavy as her little adventure had worn her out. She let out a yawn and soon she had drifted off into a sound sleep, leaving her brother alone with his thoughts. Ethan eventually went to sleep and their parents found both siblings in his bed the next morning.

Alice's mom felt a bit of joy and happiness that her two surviving children were bonding tighter than ever. It was just what they needed now. To be there for each other.

CHAPTER

SEVEN

With Halloween fast approaching and everyone at school getting ready for the local haunted house party, Alice didn't feel bad that she hadn't gotten an invite as she knew that the escapade that she and Hal were planning would be better.

Alice was in her room texting with Hal before breakfast and making plans to get back at the bullies during the local haunted house party. Hal had already sent over a list of things they'd be needing to spook the bullies at the party and Alice was getting ready to go ask her mom if she could drive her to the costume shop.

Hurrying out of her room and meeting her mother in the kitchen, Alice piped up. "Good morning Mom. Can you please take me costume shopping today?"

Alice's mom, albeit a tad bit surprised at her daughter's interest in Halloween this year, gladly obliged to take her. "Of course dear! I mean, I was always hoping to take you dress shopping, but given how weird you are, my little bat, this will do." Alice's mom smiled back at her daughter; feeling an unusual warmth inside of her as she watched Alice dart off to her room again. It was a rare sight to see Alice happy these days—almost like stumbling on a unicorn.

"Thanks Mom. I'll be out soon," Alice called out as she hurried to change her clothes.

The drive to the costume shop was mostly silent and a bit awkward as both mother and daughter wanted to talk to each other but both decided to keep mute.

In a futile attempt to drown out the deafening silence, Alice punched the buttons on the car stereo and began to navigate through the radio stations; hoping to stumble across a song that she liked.

Alice's mom watched her daughter in silence as Alice fiddled with the stereo knob, wearing a distasteful scowl on her face as she didn't get what she wanted. She eventually got pissed off then turned off the radio and slumped back in the passenger seat, staring out the window.

GIving a soft sigh, Alice's mom glanced over at her daughter and then back at the road. "Are you okay?"

"Mmm...hmmm." Alice nodded affirmatively, still staring out the window.

Her mom had that look that said she didn't really believe her daughter. "Anything you wanna get off your chest? I mean it's just us girls on this trip," Alice's mom probed further, casting a stoic glance at her daughter in the passenger seat.

Alice was already starting to feel unnerved and also slightly regretful on why she hadn't thought about the investigative journalist side of her mother whenever they were alone. She was always looking to know everything and anything going on in the kids' lives — possibly a ripple effect from Jane's death and the unspoken guilty feeling that she had failed in her duties as a mom.

"Mom, I just wanna go costume shopping. Not talk or anything. Trust me, I'm good." Alice flashed a nervous smile at her mother but her mother noticed Alice's stone cold reflection once the latter turned her face back to stare outside the window.

"I think it's time you start considering therapy again. It sure does a whole lot of good," Alice's mom steered a bend as she announced her thoughts to her daughter.

Alice was slightly befuddled at her mother's remark. She thought they were way past this topic of therapy but apparently her mother still wanted that for her. "C'mon mom! Therapy? Like seriously?!" Alice blurted out a slew of rhetorics as her mom kept driving. "Mom, you know exactly how I feel about therapy and talking to some stranger about my life." Alice groaned, hoping her mother would see reason to withdraw her statement.

Alice knew this was definitely something her mother and father had agreed on in privacy. She wanted to ask why everyone thought she was losing it and needed a therapist but after recalling her most recent outburst at the dinner table, she really couldn't blame her parents for being so concerned about the well-being of her mental health. They obviously wouldn't want a repeat of whatever happened to Jane.

Casting another glance at her daughter, Alice's mom casually retorted, "You know I had to wash your dad's shirt after your little incident with him a few nights ago. I know you were pissed off at him, but honey, your father deserves none of that. None of us do." She glanced over at a now calm and silent Alice who looked like she truly regretted tossing the takeout at her father a few nights ago.

"I'm sorry," Alice mumbled.

"It's fine, honey. I'm not the one you owe an apology to. As long as you agree to visit the therapist again. This is not up for a debate!" Alice's mom retorted emphatically and Alice lightly bumped the back of her head against the headrest in defeat.

There was no way she was talking her way out of this one. Her mom had her and had her good.

"And I want you to see the psychiatrist again. This time I think maybe we should consider those medications, mm?" She smiled amorously at her daughter, albeit Alice didn't smile back, only rolled her eyes sarcastically.

A few minutes later, Alice's mom pulled up into the parking lot of a local costume shop and Alice briefly thought about ditching her plans when she saw how crowded the store was. She remembered Hal and all they'd promised to do this Halloween and knew she couldn't disappoint him.

Suppressing her antisocial tendencies, she trudged into the store ahead of her mother and boldly did her shopping as a handful of students from her school were also present at the store with their parents. Some recognized her but Alice barely paid them any mind as she wrapped up her shopping, paid with her mom's card, and then left the costume store in a hurry.

CHAPTER

EIGHT

The next evening, Alice snuck out of the house with a trash bag filled with the costume props she had bought and headed to the haunted house to meet up with Hal. She waved frantically at him once she was close to the house and he waved back with a beaming smile. "Well good thing he isn't pacing around today," Alice mumbled to herself as she hurried towards the haunted house.

Hal also hurried towards her to help her with the hefty trash bag which housed all the scary items they needed to make the bullies piss their pants. "Wow. You sure are making a statement to these assholes this year!" Hal quipped as he emptied the sac in the haunted house and saw Alice had gotten everything he requested and more. There was a three liter jar of fake blood, fake skulls, a jagged leather face mask, and even fake stuffed bats with elongated fangs.

"Well we better get to setting everything up!" Alice chimed with glee as they both hurried into the dimly lit haunted house.

Both Hal and Alice moved from room to room; redecorating each room with grotesque costumes and spraying fake blood all over the entrance and walls. Hal produced a butcher knife at some point; coating it in the fake blood and pinning the bloodied leather face mask to the wall with the knife. Underneath the grotesque setup, he wrote the words *Keep acting tough until I carve out your face for my wall*. He made sure to scribble the inscription with the fake blood, adding the extra gruesome effect to it.

Alice began giggling and laughing at Hal's ingenuity when it came to scaring someone shitless. He ripped a fake skeleton in half; coating the torso part with the fake blood before dressing the skeleton in a torn dirty shirt and leaving it in a poorly drawn penta-gram right in the middle of one of the biggest rooms in the haunted house. He also left a knife stuck to the skull of the skeleton; prying the jaw half open to give it that horrific effect. Alice was laughing as she followed Hal around the haunted house and watched him retouch the place to suit his taste.

"Haha, I can't wait to see the looks on their faces when they walk in for their party." Alice laughed out loud when Hal was finally done with redecorating the last room; fake blood was splattered on his shirt and sleeves, but his beaming grin made Alice at ease as they locked eyes for a bit and smiled at each other.

Glancing back at the room to behold their work, Hal wore a proud smirk on his face as he turned back to behold Alice. "This is truly wonderful," he quipped in a soft but firm tone, his face lit up like a kid at Christmas. "I never could have imagined myself having so much fun pranking suckers," Hal added with a chortle and Alice felt butterflies flutter in the pit of her stomach while her knees went weak.

She stared deep into Hal's eyes and he did the same. Both of them subconsciously took a step forward to bridge the gap between them and in a flash, they'd meshed their lips together with eyes tightly shut. Although the kiss was short, both parties felt sparks fly as they gently pulled their lips apart and smiled sweetly at each other.

Alice had gone red in the face as she couldn't even recall the last time she kissed a boy. She tried glancing up into Hal's chiseled face and beady eyes but she just couldn't this time, blushing uncontrollably like a girl having her first crush.

Hal also looked a bit embarrassed but tried to mask it by holding Alice's arm gently. They locked eyes again and felt another kiss was forthcoming when a loud banging sound elicited from a distant room in the haunted house, echoing loudly around the house and startling both of them to attention.

"Did you hear that?" Alice cast a sweeping gaze all around and then up at Hal who had a scrunched look on his face as he tried to pinpoint where the strange noise had come from.

"Yes, I did," Hal replied in a hushed tone as he let go of Alice before walking past her towards the entrance of the room. He peered out into the dimly lit hallway and then almost in a flash, he reeled his head back with eyes wide. "Ghost," he whispered with all seriousness to an observant Alice.

Thinking Hal was trying to play a fast one on her, Alice scoffed and rolled her eyes. "Yeah right, Hal. Ghosts indeed!" She scoffed as she also peeped out into the hallway. Although Alice couldn't pick anything out in the dark, she felt the same eerie chill taut had enveloped her at the park that night to crawl up her spine as a silent gust of wind swept past her. Quickly pulling back into the room, Alice glanced back at Hal, her expressive wide eyes saying much more than her lips could utter at the moment. She wanted to ask Hal if it was a good or evil ghost lurking but knew that would only exacerbate her fears. It was somewhat eerily hilarious to Alice that the haunted house which they'd thought needed more haunting looks, was actually haunted in the real sense.

"You saw it, too?" Hal asked rhetorically with a smile once he noticed Alice's reaction.

Alice didn't know how to reply and just stared up at him with a slackened jaw. She supposed Hal had been able to see the ghost because he was more spiritually awake than she. Nevertheless, it was almost impossible to shake off the trepidation that they weren't alone anymore as Alice felt the cold wind surge up her spine again. Something was definitely here now.

"C'mon! Let's communicate with the spirit of our dead siblings again!" Hal piped up as he hurried over to where his backpack lay and fished out the Ouija board. Alice felt a pit in her stomach as she watched him spread out the board. She really wasn't ready for this today.

Alice gulped a hard lump down her dry throat at Hal's suggestion of consulting with the spirits of their dead siblings again. As much as she still had a plethora of questions plaguing her since her last talk with her dead sister, Alice still hadn't fully gotten over the experience. Plus, the insinuation that her sister had suffered before death made it even more eerie to carry on.

However, there was also something about how easily consulting with spirits of the dead came to Hal. It was almost as if he did this in his spare time, resulting in loads of experience regarding the nether realm.

Glancing at the time on her illuminated cell phone screen, Alice nervously squinted up at Hal's expectant gleaming eyes under the lowlights of the room they were in. "I'm sorry Hal, my parents are out and I'm babysitting Ethan tonight," she replied in a casual lie in order to avert taking part in his random suggestion that had suddenly ruined the mood.

There was a tense moment of silence between both of them as Hal stared in an almost transfixed gaze deep into Alice's eyes, making her grow even more nervous at the moment. "Hey, are you okay, Hal?" Alice muttered with a slowly stretching arm towards his face in an attempt to break the awkward silence.

Knocking her arm away with the back of his palm, a visibly annoyed Hal snapped back at her, "You're lying!"

Alice was almost knocked off her feet by how confident his reply was. She felt a sharp ache in her chest that she'd have to stand by this lie of hers regardless if he believed her or not. Regardless of how much it hurt to lie to him, she wasn't meditating with spirits tonight and would do whatever it took to keep it that way. "Ow, Hal, that hurt." Alice groaned as she clutched her wrist and stared at Hal in fright.

"You're just like the rest of them at school, huh," Hal started off with a growl.

"Hal," Alice interrupted in an attempt to stop him from saying what they both would regret.

"What?!" Hal sniggered with furrowed brows as he took a step forward and grabbed Alice by her already hurting wrist, gripping tightly and staring into her eyes while Alice grew red in the face from stifling a cry that was about to burst out.

She couldn't believe how scared and heartbroken she was at the same time. Her wrist hurt incredibly badly from Hal's grip and she couldn't yank him off no matter how she pulled.

"You're scared your cover's been blown? I always knew you were just out for yourself and no one..."

"HAL!!!" Alice screamed in a shrill cry, interrupting Hal from finishing. "You're hurting me!" Alice sobbed.

Suddenly, like he'd been having an out-of-body experience, Hal swiftly yanked his arm away from hers, revealing a fresh bruise around her wrist.

Another eerie silence elapsed as tears sluiced down Alice's red face. She hurriedly wiped them off with the back of her palms before clearing her throat. "I think I should leave now," she piped up emphatically, staring at Hal's expressionless eyes which looked frighteningly cold.

Without uttering a word, Hal watched as Alice backtracked out of the room before briskly walking down the hallway where they'd both sworn to see a ghost.

Alice walked as fast as her legs could carry her; sobbing and rubbing on her bruised wrist as she walked. *Why did Hal act the way he did? Why was he unapologetic? Was he really responsible for his brother's death?* All these were the plethora of questions plaguing Alice on her way home and regardless of not having the answers to all of them, she knew for certain that Hal had hurt her. It was even worse that he didn't bat an eye about the bruise he gave her.

Once she arrived home, Alice quickly wiped off the tears from her face and tried to pull the sleeve of her sweatshirt all the way down her wrists in order to cover the bruise. She walked in through the front door to see her dad and mom seated in the living room.

"Hey Alice. Where've you been?" her father asked in a friendly cheer like the last incident between them hadn't even happened.

Trying to hide her arms, Alice replied, "Oh nowhere. Just out studying. With friends," she quipped her reply in near stutters.

"Oh, alright," her dad replied and settled back on the couch.

"Are you sure everything's alright, Alice?" her mom asked in an inquisitive tone, stopping Alice in her tracks, right as she was about to storm off.

"Mmm hmmm," Alice nodded affirmatively, flashing a fake faint smile of reassurance at her mother, which really didn't have its desired effect as her mother still watched her with curious eyes until she disappeared into her room.

Alone in her room, Alice stripped off her clothes before walking into the bathroom. She turned on the shower and let out a soft sigh as the warm water flowed down her body in satisfying beads, offering her a soothing and relaxing feeling. She shut her eyes and leaned against the wall as she let the events of the evening stream through her mind.

Suddenly Alice's eyes flew wide open at the sound of an eerie whooshing noise behind her. She frantically dried the water from her eyes as she glanced around the bathroom. Unable to see anything, Alice let out a soft sigh of relief. She guessed she was overly tense over nothing as she proceeded to lean against the tiled wall and let the warm shower trickle down her body. Then the whooshing sound echoed again, this time closer to her ears with that particular, familiar eerie chill from the park.

"Hello? Anybody there?" Alice called out with a thumping heart as she wiped her sight clear again but still saw nothing. She hastily grabbed her towel and began to dab her body dry as she realized she couldn't continue with the shower. She swore she could still feel the shadows from the haunted house following her. *Maybe I do need those meds.* She sat dejectedly at the edge of her bed wrapped in just her towel, wet hair splayed across her face as she stared off into nothingness, her mind a wreckage of inordinate thoughts.

CHAPTER

NINE

Alice felt Hal's eyes on her from behind as she feigned attention at the science teacher in the laboratory. Casually glancing over her shoulder, she truly caught Hal's cold eyes locked on every single movement of hers like a heat seeking missile would its target. Shrugging away the feeling of uneasiness that raised the hair on her neck, Alice pulled her gaze away and muttered to herself. "Weirdo!"

Her seat partner glanced at her as it was rather surprising hearing the class weirdo call someone else a weirdo. It had been a whole week since Alice and Hal last spoke after the incident at the haunted house. Alice had decided to stay away from him, which was easier than she realized. She realized her mental health and grip on reality was rapidly declining with him around.

The bell rang out, signaling lunch break, and Alice was more than pleased to sprint out of the laboratory with her book bag. She started alone down the hallways and she could feel a sea of eyes trail her movements as some of her bullies wanted to taunt her but the fear of Hal kept them at bay. Alice could see the fear in their eyes as she stalked past them and walked into the girls restroom. She chose her favorite stall but realized it was occupied by two teenagers making out.

"Get out of here and go eat at the cafeteria like everyone else, weirdo," a girl yelled out from the locked stall as an infuriated Alice yanked at the handle.

"Well how about you two quit fucking in public bathrooms and go get a room," Alice yelled back in frustration as she kicked the door and then walked away angrily. Fuming, she made her way out of the building and towards the open field. She found her way underneath the bleachers where Hal was peacefully seated with a half smoked joint between his fingertips.

Hal nonchalantly glanced up at Alice's dark silhouette once she covered the shade of the sun with her body. "Hey," he casually quipped then took another drag of his joint.

Feeling more pissed off that Hal didn't even deem it fit to apologize for his last outburst, Alice let out a scoff of pure disbelief and it was clearly written on her face. "Are you even serious right now? Hey?" she piped up rhetorically as Hal just kept mute. A tentative moment of silence ensued as Alice looked down on this particular boy and wondered why it had to be him. "I don't think I can do this anymore," Alice blurted to break the silence and startled Hal who turned to squarely face her with red dilated pupils.

"What do you mean by that?" Hal's voice trembled a bit in his vocal cords as he spoke up for the first time in a long time.

Alice couldn't deny that she'd missed listening to him talk but she just couldn't carry on with their toxic relationship which was starting to take its toll on her grip on reality. "I mean I'm breaking up whatever this thing is between us. I just can't carry on like this, Hal. I'm sorry, but I'm not looking to lose my mind. Imagine what that'll do to my brother."

Hal's eyes blinked rapidly at the mention of her brother and Alice felt her heart ache as she stood before him to break his heart.

In a surprising twist, Hal's face contorted in a smirk after Alice was done. "Yeah. You can go on ahead and save your sanity while I lose my life. Fair bargain, if you ask me," he quipped stoically as he stared long and hard at his sizzling joint before pulling another long hard drag.

Still struggling to process what she'd just heard, Alice moved a step forward. "I'm sorry, what now?" she stuttered.

"You heard me," Hal glanced up at her with an almost maniacal smile. "I'll off myself if you leave me," he said the words with such levity, almost like they didn't hold much weight and that they wouldn't bring many tragic memories to Alice.

Crumbling on her knees and grabbing Hal by the collar of his shirt, a gobsmacked and equally frightened Alice held onto him tightly as she locked eyes with him. "Have you lost yourself, Hal? How could you say such a thing?" Alice's voice was quivering as she spoke each word, staring into Hal's eyes and hoping he didn't mean what he just said. She suddenly felt an eerie trepidation envelop her that if anything were to happen to Hal, she would have herself to blame for life and she doubted if she would be able to live on with such guilt.

"Then don't leave me, Alice, you're all I've got," Hal calmly retorted, staring into Alice's eyes that already had tears welling up in them. He realized how much she was in love with him as she was visibly shaken and discombobulated at his threat to take his own life.

"I won't, Hal. I won't!" Alice threw her arms around Hal's body; pulling him for a tight hug and felt the warmth of his body, plus the aroma of his joint awash all over him. "Please don't ever say something like that again." She sobbed softly into his chest.

Hal gently reached up with one palm and then began smoothing Alice's blonde hair. "I'm sorry. I won't say it again, I promise," Hal muttered as he calmed her sobs.

In order to make things better, Alice pulled back before wiping the tears off her face as she looked into Hal's eyes. "Let's do it tonight," she piped up in an enthusiastic whisper. "Let's talk to our dead siblings just like you suggested," she added, gently holding Hal's hands.

Hal finally cracked a smile— a real one at that as he pulled Alice closer and hugged her tightly. Alice was glad he'd stopped talking about killing himself as she never wanted to ever hear him say such again.

As much as she was annoyed with him hurting her and not apologizing, she just couldn't lose him. Being away from him for the last week had proven that to her, she didn't want to be away from him.

CHAPTER

TEN

Alice found herself trudging through the narrow pathway in the woods which led towards the park as she didn't want to risk either of her returning parents running into her if she took the main streets. Ever since making her promise to Hal a few hours ago at school, Alice couldn't seem to get her mind off the plethora of questions she had lined up for Jane tonight. She had even written them down on her cellphone's notepad as she didn't want to forget a thing.

She wouldn't need the notes as she had memorized everything by the time she arrived at the meeting point to see Hal staring up at the sky; the Ouija board already spread out beside him like a chess maester awaiting a worthy opponent. "Hey," Alice trailed off, pulling on her hood to reveal her face as she settled beside Hal on the bench, taking a stoic glance at the Ouija board between them.

"It's a full moon tonight," Hal mumbled with his head still craned up to the sky. For the first time, Alice realized the moon had actually come out to play in all its spherical glory, hanging between the clouds like one could reach up and snatch it. They both gawked in silence at the bright moon illuminating the night sky before Alice cleared her throat to signal her impatience. Hal was starting to act weird again.

Slowly pulling his gaze down and smiling at Alice, Hal whispered, "Hey...how're you?"

Alice felt her stomach tingle with butterflies at his question and she couldn't help but beam a brief smile as she replied, "I'm fine. You're so sweet." She reached out to pat his cheek and then let go with a sigh. "C'mon, I'm ready." She cast a glance down at the Ouija board and then back up at Hal.

"Alright, you know what to do." Hal readjusted on the bench as he watched Alice shut her eyes, take deep breaths and call out her dead sister's name three times into the night. This time, there was a quick reply; a gust of cold wind whooshing through the woods and bursting out into the park— shaking the trees of their autumn leaves that both Hal and Alice had to shield their eyes as it swept up to them. Everything went silent again and Hal had that look that said there was a third party present.

Swallowing a hard lump down her dry throat, Alice swiftly recalled the first question on her list. "Are you alright, Jane?" she called out into the night. The planchette began moving around at her question; swiftly spelling out the words; *Been through worse, still feel like shit.* Alice couldn't help but giggle out loud with a shaky tone as she perfectly resonated with her sister's sarcasm. Even in death, she still kept her charming sense of humor.

Hal watched as Alice's face turned red and she fought to fight back a bead of tear from escaping her eyes. "Oh god, Alice, you've barely asked her anything!" Alice chided herself as she sniffled, wiped the tear with the back of her palm and then chortled softly again. Suddenly, Alice's facial features contorted from that of a beaming, blushing smile to a disturbed frown as the next question popped up in her mind.

She took a deep breath before letting it out. "Why did you do it,

Jane? Tell me why you did that to yourself." Alice paused to catch her breath as she ran her palms through her ponytail. "I'll never have closure til I know why you did it, Jane. So you can either tell me or torture me more by remaining silent. Your call." Alice sniffled with a coy shrug. She glanced over at Hal who gave her a subtle nod of approval with fixated eyes.

The planchette moved a few letters before stopping—almost like the force that propelled it was hesitant. Both Alice's and Hal's attention were focused on the board as it paused its movements then rearranged back to its default mode. Alice let out a frustrated groan. "C'mon, Jane, spit it out," she whispered emphatically at the Ouija board.

The planchette resumed its movement, swiftly spelling out a slew of words that both teenagers had to swiftly keep up with. *Dad started touching me years ago. Mom didn't believe. Couldn't take it anymore. Off myself.*

Alice's face horribly scrunched up and she felt her stomach hurting as she read out the words on the planchette. She stared wide-eyed up at Hal and could immediately see he had a sorry and startled look as he equally couldn't believe what he'd just read. "This can't be. No. Jane, please tell me what you mean by touching." Alice's voice quivered as she hoped she misinterpreted what the board had just spelt out as the words descrambled.

Dad sneaking into my room to rape me since I was twelve.

Alice literally felt the world around her crumble into a debris of nothingness as Jane's spirit wasn't lacking in profanity either; blatantly spelling out the abuse she'd suffered at the hands of their father before taking her own life. Alice was both befuddled and discombobulated by the revelation. Her perfect father was really a beast behind closed doors and Jane had been his unfortunate prey. She cupped her face to stifle a shrill cry that leapt out from deep within her and in a flash, Hal shut the Ouija board and pulled her close, holding her quivering body as she sobbed into his body.

"I'm sorry your sister had to experience such pain. I'm so so sorry," Hal whispered into a sobbing Alice's ear and like on cue, she bawled out into uncontrollable bouts of tears while he comforted her tightly.

ELEVEN

"Alice, your teacher called, she said you've been acting distracted lately and to ask if everything's alright with you," Alice's dad asked as she had been summoned to the living room after the terms results were in. Her brother had done well but Alice's results were a total disaster. She'd even missed a couple of exams which had her parents worried.

"Alice, dear, if there's anything troubling you, you know you can tell us about it, right," Alice's mom asked in a sweet loving tone.

Sitting opposite her parents, Alice stared blankly at them; from her mother to her father. She was trying her best to mask a trickle of disgust that struggled to creep up on her face whenever she met her father's gaze or heard his voice echo up. He was borderline repulsive to her but she knew she couldn't explain what she'd found out without looking like she'd lost her mind. Watching him act like a priestly saint was disgusting for Alice and she tightened her lips together as she listened to him speak again.

"Alice, your grades came in, and believe me, it has us quite worried," Alice's dad continued, tossing a file on the center table before him.

Alice stared blankly at the file which she knew was her grades for the term then looked away. School was the last thing on her mind now.

"I mean, this is the worst you've performed ever. Not even after..." he trailed off as Alice's mom gently touched him on the knee with a knowing glance. He paused to be careful with his words after a deep sigh. "Alice, we're just worried about you, that's all. We are your parents and we know something's wrong somewhere, you're just being secretive about it."

"You remember what we said about keeping secrets, honey, we're a family," Alice's mom chipped in, trying her best to get her daughter to open up to them.

Letting out a scoff with an exaggerated expression of embarrassment, Alice retorted, "Seriously, guys? I flunk just one term and I'm getting all this heat?!"

"We just want to know..." Alice's mom tried to interject.

"NOTHING IS WRONG!" Alice stared at her mother as she yelled emphatically to bring the conversation to a brief, awkward halt.

Gently picking up the file from the table, her father broke the tentative silence with a firm tone. "Seems whatever this is, is quite personal seeing as you can't talk to your mom or me about it." He stared at her stoically and sighed. "Well since you can't answer us, then maybe you shouldn't go to tonight's Halloween party," he stated with a tone of finality.

Alice completely lost it at this point. The Halloween party was her only chance to get back at the bullies plus also try to mediate with her sister using the Ouija board. Hal would be waiting for her. She definitely didn't want to disappoint him. Springing up from where she was seated, Alice roared manically at both of her parents. "You both are selfish!" Alice yelled with disdain at her parents.

"Alice!" Her father yelled at her in a firm tone that he thought would cool her off but only seemed to further infuriate her as she fixated her rage filled eyes on him.

"And you! I know what you did to my sister! I KNOW WHAT YOU DID TO JANE!" Alice yelled out manically, pointing at her father.

Alice's mom stood up from the couch, reaching for her daughter who looked like she'd lost it. "Alice, honey, please calm down. What you're saying doesn't make sense," she tried to placate her daughter's rage.

Yanking her arm away from her mother's grasp, Alice yelled at her befuddled father. "YOU HURT HER! NIGHT AFTER NIGHT, YOU HURT HER! You can't lie because the board told me everything." She sniffled after a tirade of yelling out her voice.

Ethan had been attracted downstairs by the yelling and stood in the doorway now. "Yes, it's true. Alice has been talking to sissy and sissy's been telling her things," Ethan blurted out to break the stunned silence that had enveloped the living room, save for Alice's snuggling and sobbing.

"What? Oh god, no!" Alice's mom looked troubled now, reaching for her daughter's face and gently clutching it in her hands. She feared her daughter had spiraled downhill and needed urgent help. "Honey, I think she's sick!" Alice's mom turned to her husband with tears welled up in her eyes as her hands trembled around Alice's face.

Her dad had stealthily dialed 911 on his cellphone.

Stepping back in disbelief, Alice yanked her mother's hands away from her face. "What? You don't believe me? You think I'm sick?!" Alice stared at her mother in shock. She glanced over at her father as he began to explain his daughter was having *hallucinations* about her dead sister. Alice couldn't believe how quickly her parents had put the mental health spin on the true story she'd been told by her sister's spirit.

"Alice, just take it easy and we'll get through this together," her father tried to placate her after his brief call.

Alice tried to leave the room but her father ordered Ethan to shut the door and stay out. Within fifteen minutes, the door burst open as two policemen and a female doctor with two male nurses walked into the living room.

"Don't worry honey, everything will be fine," Alice's mom tried to pacify her as Alice began to panic and hyperventilate at the sight of the unknown faces.

One nurse grabbed her and before she knew it she was forced into a straight jacket and put on a stretcher to take her out of the house. While wriggling and yelling out on the stretcher, Alice felt a sharp sting on her neck as she was administered a powerful dose of sedatives that knocked her unconscious right away. Her parents and brother watched with tears in their eyes as she was loaded up into an ambulance and driven off to be administered at the hospital's psychiatric unit.

CHAPTER
TWELVE

"Urgghh....shhhiittt...." Alice groaned in subtle agony as she blinked her eyes awake to stare at the hovering halogen light above her bed in the hospital's psychiatric ward. Ever since her arrival at the psych ward, everything had been a blur to Alice as she was constantly being heavily sedated, albeit she got the help she needed.

Nevertheless, she still felt angry that no one had taken her seriously concerning the revelations from the Ouija board. Squinting at the bright light as she tried to keep herself awake this time, Alice's concentration was broken off by the soothing voice of a teenage girl beside her.

"The medications suck, don't they?" the teenage girl quipped in an almost eerie voice, pulling Alice's gaze from the ceiling, towards her.

Glancing over at the girl who just spoke, Alice noticed it was a girl about sixteen years old with a skinny frame and a shaved head. There was something cat-like about the way the skinny bald girl sprang up on her bed before crawling closer to stare into Alice's face from her own bed.

Alice groaned softly, musing within herself at how she didn't want to converse with another weirdo at the psych ward but something about the observant girl just made her at ease. *Plus, it wouldn't hurt to make a friend at the psych ward.* "What's your name?" Alice groaned at the wide eyed, bald girl.

"Chelsie," the girl replied with equally rapt attention, staring unabashedly at Alice from her bed nearby.

"Nice to meet you Chelsie, I'm Alice," Alice retorted with a mild cough.

Chelsie sprang off her bed in that cat-like fashion, appearing beside Alice's bed in a flash.

Alice was slightly startled at how lightly the frail girl moved on her feet. It was almost as astonishing as it was frightening.

Standing beside Alice's bed, Chelsie acted like she was going to sniff around Alice, almost like a dog sniffing out an intruder in the vicinity.

Alice had a mortified look on her face as she watched the strange girl hover around her for a bit before pulling back with a bothered scrunch to her face.

"There's something dark around you," Chelsie leaned down to whisper to Alice.

Alice felt the hairs at the nape of her neck stand at the girl's assertion but waved it off with a groan. "Yeah, right, there's something all right. Same thing that made my parents haul my ass to this place!" Alice scoffed in nonchalant reply. She paused to groan at the ceiling again before groggily sitting up in her bed.

Chelsie's eyes were still fixated on Alice as she watched her struggle. "He's your boyfriend, isn't he?" Chelsie asked randomly from out of the blue, briefly startling Alice.

"Look, Chelsie, I don't know if you've been through my file but I really don't have the energy for this back and forth right now, okay? My head keeps banging like a high school band ever since I opened up my eyes so please, just, shhh," Alice groaned her reply at Chelsie, unable to keep up with the plethora of questions from the inquisitive cat girl.

A tentative eerie silence elapsed between both girls but Chelsie's eyes remained fixated on Alice's, almost like she was scanning her soul with her deep searching eyes. "Alright! It's your funeral!" Chelsie piped up with a coy shrug and an almost disturbing smirk. "Just be careful with that Hal guy, okay?" she whispered rhetorically before pacing back to her bed and getting in.

Alice's breath seized for a tentative bit at Chelsie's statement and she watched the cat-like girl hop in her bed. Alice wondered if Chelsie had somehow gone through her file but she still knew Hal was her secret and just barely a handful of people knew they were together besides her schoolmates.

"Thanks," Alice muttered softly in reply as her mind plunged into deep thoughts about Hal. She realized she'd missed him so much and the days without him were grueling as they were long, even though she spent those past days in a drugged fog.

A FEW DAYS LATER, still at the psych ward and Alice was truly starting to lose it. She still hadn't found a way to contact Hal and it was destroying her. She missed him dearly and wished she could see him again as she knew he'd have also missed her as well.

"You wanna talk to him, don't you?" Chelsie muttered to Alice one day while they were alone in their ward after a nurse's exit.

Alice paused from running her palms through her unkept and tousled blonde hair and stared wide eyed at Chelsie. "Yes, yes! But the fucking doctors won't let me have any phone calls. They said my parents specifically requested I talk to nobody besides them." Alice let out a groan of frustration as she slumped back against the bed frame, staring stoically up in his ceiling and wondering if she'd ever see her heartthrob, Hal, again.

"Oh, that's sad," Chelsie replied softly before another tentative silence elapsed. "Maybe you can use my call. I never have reason to call my parents despite how much they want me to." Chelsie shrugged casually as she nibbled on a finger and then clawed her wrist to check the other fingernails. "Or use my cell phone that they don't know I have!"

Sitting up in a flash on her bed, Alice's eyes beamed wide with glimpses of hope. "Please, Chelsie. If you've got it and really don't mind, then let me have it please!" Alice retorted with eyes wide and expectant.

Chelsie let off a wry smug as she reached underneath her pillow and pulled out a burner cell phone which she handed to an anxious Alice.

"Thank you so much!" Alice snatched the phone and then made a hasty beeline for the restroom, frantically punching in Hal's number and dialing it. In the privacy of the restroom, she held the ringing phone against her ear, listening to each agonizingly painful ring that went unanswered. Alice swallowed a hard lump in her dry throat as she paused to hurriedly send a text to the number, telling Hal to pick up that it was her. She dialed his number over and over again but all she got was a static ring that went on for what felt like forever. She wiped off a hot bead of tears from her eyes after the endless calls came to an end with no reply.

CHAPTER
THIRTEEN

It was Alice's discharge day from the psychiatric unit and she couldn't wait for her parents to come get her. It had been a grueling couple of weeks and Alice wouldn't wish this experience on her enemy. She said goodbye to her only friend at the facility—Chelsie, before heading out to meet her parents in the driveway.

Alice put up a relaxed demeanor in front of her parents now, no longer bawling at the things she'd found out about her father and dead sister. She guessed there would be another way at getting revenge for her sister besides being the raging yelling girl who everyone thought had lost her mind.

During the silent ride home, Alice thought about Hal and wondered what he'd been up to since she had been away. Maybe he'd consulted with the spirit of her dead sister without her and found out more family secrets or perhaps, he had simply moved on and found another girl. Both instances were quite troubling to Alice who had gotten nothing more than a text message from Hal after days of love bombing him with Chelsie's phone.

"Are you alright, honey?" Alice's mom asked from the passenger seat, glancing behind with a beaming smile at her daughter.

Knowing she had to put up the perfect act to avoid getting sent back to the godforsaken psych ward, Alice copied her mother's beaming smile. "Yes, Mom, I'm fine." She nodded affirmatively and her father smiled at her through the rear view mirror.

The family soon arrived home a few minutes later and as soon as Alice stepped out on the lawn, she realized just how much she'd missed home as a wave of nostalgia enveloped her.

"You're not coming in yet?" Alice's mom asked from the front door as Alice remained rooted to a spot, glancing at the building like it was her first time seeing it.

"In a minute!" Alice vocally retorted as her mom and dad disappeared into the house. Taking a deep breath, Alice began casually walking around the house. She was almost to the backyard when she heard a faint male grunt followed by a clanking of stone against glass panes. Carefully sticking her head around into the backyard, Alice's heart skipped multiple beats as she came face to face with Hal. He was flagrantly tossing stones up at her window and had even succeeded in leaving a visible dent that might eventually shatter if he kept up his tossing.

"Hal?" Alice called out, almost in disbelief as she feared the meds might still be doing a number on her with the hallucinations.

Glancing over in shock at the familiar voice that had just called out his name, Hal let out a muffled gasp once he set eyes on a red faced Alice, standing a few meters away from him with tears welling up in her pretty eyes.

"Oh my goodness, Alice. It's really you!" Hal charged forward in a flash before he then wrapped his arms around her in a tight bear hug.

Alice was torn between pushing Hal off or just staying put. She wanted to ask him why he hadn't called back or even visited at all. She wanted to tell him how lonely she'd been most nights, crying herself to sleep with him being the last person on her mind.

Hal let out a sniffle as he tightly held onto Alice for what felt like forever. He pulled back and Alice could see he equally had a reddened face and tears welled up in his eyes as well. It both hurt and fascinated her to see Hal this vulnerable as she'd never seen him shed a tear in her presence — not even for his deceased brother. "I thought you left me." Hal sniffled to break the long silence between them after they ended the long hug. "I was ready to kill myself," he added.

Reaching up to cup his face between her palms, Alice steadied Hal's gaze into her eyes. "I would never ever leave you, Hal. I feared you had moved on when I didn't hear back from YOU," Alice retorted in almost a nervous chortle-cry state, wiping off Hal's tears as she grazed his cheeks with her tender fingers.

Hal shook his head. "No, I would never do that to you."

Alice felt a warm sensation in her heart at his reassurance. She flung her arms around his shoulders and he pulled her close by the small of her waistline, planting his lips on hers as they engaged in a sensual French kiss that lasted for a long time. Alice moaned softly into the kiss, clutching tightly onto Hal's neck while he kept his arms cradled around her waist as they kissed. They finally pulled away for need of air and stared at each other amorously with affection filled eyes.

"I love you, Hal," Alice whispered in a faint voice.

Gently planting a kiss on her forehead, Hal smiled as he replied, "I love you, too, Alice." He held her tightly for another couple of minutes before slowly pulling back and smiling at her. "C'mon, let's get you inside before your parents send out a search party." Holding her by her arm, Hal led Alice towards the back entrance and Alice couldn't help but giggle softly at his remark. She'd sure missed everything about this boy and wasn't letting anything get in the way of their love again— not even what her dead sister's spirit would tell her.

CHAPTER

FOURTEEN

Alice woke up to a faint knock outside her bedroom window early the next morning. Groaning awake, she slid the curtains aside to see a smiling Hal at the other side of the window, a box of pizza held up invitingly in one hand. Alice smiled at how much she'd missed good junk food and how Hal had just known what to get her. Her mother had tried her repulsive cooking last night and just as always, her father snuck her Panda Express after she'd endured the dinner.

"Hey, you gonna open up or what?" Hal whispered while mouthing emphatically and waving the box of pizza in the air as he took a frantic sweep of the backyard to be sure no one was coming.

Giggling at how cute he looked flustered and slightly frightened, Alice scrambled for the window and slid it open, pulling Hal's face close to hers and kissing him deeply before he got a chance to sneak into the room.

"This...this is really cute, Alice, but I don't want to get shot in the ass by your dad," Hal whispered as he broke the kiss, causing Alice to giggle and move aside so he could slither in.

She shut the window after glancing out to see a neighbor's dog had been silently watching the entire time. Alice felt it was strange that such a noisy dog would choose to remain silent when it mattered the most. Whatever it was, she was glad the dog hadn't caused a ruckus this morning. She watched in faint surprise as the dog suddenly darted off in the opposite direction with its tail between its legs.

"You okay? Someone there?" Hal moved towards the window, holding Alice from behind.

Swiftly turning around with a gleeful smile, Alice let the curtains shut. "Nothing. Just a silly dog." She grinned at Hal before kissing him deeply; sighing and moaning into his mouth as his warm breath washed over the insides of her mouth while their tongues danced in snake-like fashion. "I missed you," Alice moaned softly after the kiss which had lasted for a few minutes. She gently leaned against Hal's chest and muttered softly, "I missed you so much it started to hurt thinking about you."

"Shhh...it's okay. I wish I could tell you how miserable the days were without you," Hal whispered in her ear. "The good thing now is that we're together and nothing is going to change that. Hmm?" He smiled at her and then planted a soft kiss on her forehead.

Alice felt a flutter of butterflies in her stomach as she smiled up at Hal before pulling him towards the bed. "C'mon, this pizza smells delicious." Alice giggled as she sat on the bed while Hal snatched up the pizza box then sat on the bed.

They both ate to their fill, Alice eating more to Hal's amazement. When they were done, they both curled up in a ball on the bed with Hal cradling Alice from behind as they each enjoyed their company, albeit drowned in their individual thoughts.

"I don't know how much longer I can keep up this act..." Alice trailed off in a daze.

"What act?" Hal's head perked up behind Alice's and she turned her face to meet his. She had suddenly gone red in the face.

"Acting like my family is normal and my dad isn't a monster," she sputtered in a whisper as she broke down in soft sobs, recalling everything the Ouija board had revealed to her that night.

"Hey, we'll find a way around this, I promise." Hal held her tightly to himself as she sobbed against his body. "You just have to promise me not to go off on him again or else they'll send you away to that hellhole for longer. Not like I would let them though..." he trailed off in such a manner that made Alice glance up at him with red glossy eyes. He wiped her eyes then flashed her a smile which she mirrored faintly.

"You're so sweet," Alice replied. "And yes, I promise not to do anything stupid. At least for now." She sighed then rubbed her eyes. A tentative silence elapsed before she piped up softly. "Tell me about the Halloween party. Tell me you still set off all our little traps even while I was locked up. I mean, come on, Hal, you couldn't think I'd miss that." Her demeanor suddenly switched to half excitement as she wanted to hear all about their Halloween prank.

Chortling softly at the recollection, Hal was glad she'd brought something up to lighten up the mood again. "You should have seen the faces of the kids at school when they followed the trail of blood all the way to the pentagram and the ripped skeleton." He paused to laugh again and Alice couldn't help but giggle along with him as she imagined the look on their faces. "Oh man, I wish I had gotten videos. A few of them actually pissed themselves." He laughed heartily and Alice burst out in a louder laughter. "It was a wonderful experience. Just that you were missing," Hal trailed off at the end of his story, causing Alice to blush bright red again.

"Don't worry we'll get 'em next time. Together!" She leaned in to plant a quick kiss on his lips but Hal held her firmly by her waist, holding her to himself so she giggled softly into his mouth as he didn't let go of her. She moaned a soft, "Stop...," followed by soft erotic moans as Hal's tongue explored deep inside her mouth while his hands began to erratically roam all around her scantily covered body in the silk nightgown she had on. Alice's moans tuned up a notch once Hal groped her left breast, kneading softly at the mound and setting her on fire. She moaned louder into the kiss, grabbing Hal's exploring hands and trailing his expert movements on her body.

Alice was about to guide Hal's strong hand in between her thighs when he suddenly pulled away from the kiss and yanked his arm away from her body, startling Alice.

Hal suddenly had a frightened look on his face before he turned around, turning his back to Alice and mumbling out like he was in deep regret. "No, no. No! I can't do it! I can't do it again," Hal muttered out to an astonished Alice's hearing.

She could barely make sense of what he was saying before he sprang up from the bed and dashed out the window in a flash, not offering Alice any explanation for the sudden change of his mood. Alice was heartbroken, and even worse, she felt like a rejected slut. She cried herself to sleep as she tried Hal's number endless times only to get his voicemail.

CHAPTER
FIFTEEN

S trolling down the school's hallway with her earphones plugged in and blasting Nirvana, Alice noticed the sea of eyes trailing her every step but shrugged it off as just another day. Today's stares seemed to be awkwardly longer and were accompanied by grouped hushing and frequent gesticulations towards her though. Not being new to the awkward stares and jeers from bullies, Alice tried to shrug off the trepidation that this was something worse. Everyone looked at her like they'd found out some terrible secret about her or like she was heading to the admin office to pick up her expulsion letter. Regardless, Alice tried to shrug it off as one of such days where the bullies just had to talk about her. *It was all good as long as they didn't approach.*

During her classes, she noticed the awkward stares and whispers continued with a few of the girls swiftly turning their faces away once Alice matched their intense gawking. Taking her mind off the disturbing sea of eyes trailing her every movement, Alice reached into her book bag for her cellphone and realized it would soon be lunch break.

It had been a few days since Hal's strange breakdown at her

house and despite sending numerous texts and leaving him count-less voicemails, Hal had simply replied with a text saying he was sorry and would make it up to her. She hadn't heard from him since then and he hadn't even returned her text when she had asked if he was coming to school today.

The depressing feeling of her former life had started to creep in slowly and the stares from her classmates weren't helping either. Finally the bell rang loudly, liberating the class of students to throng out into the hallway. Alice got up and approached one of the girls she'd caught staring at her during the class. She thought if the girl wanted to stare, she might as well help. "Excuse me, but have you seen Hal today?" Alice asked in the best friendly tone she could conjure.

Her question brought another renewed sea of eyes towards her and this time they were mostly girls. "Yeah? What would he want with you?" one girl asked with a scorn on her face and the rest of the girls burst out laughing at Alice's expense.

Alice felt a gut wrenching feeling in the pit of her stomach as this was the exact reason she hated socializing with anyone. Humans were cruel and basically assholes. Her rage came out as tears of anger and pain quickly welled up in her eyes. Not wanting a drop to escape her eyes, Alice snatched her book bag and bolted out of the class-room, sobbing as she hurriedly trudged down the hallway with another sea of eyes trailing her.

Alice was heartbroken and afraid that Hal had been spreading cruel rumors about her which would explain the stranger stares she'd been receiving all day. Crying and sobbing, Alice made her way out of the building and headed for the bleachers. She found herself a cozy spot underneath and continued sobbing with her knees clutched up to her red face.

A few minutes later, a silhouette greeted Alice as Hal emerged from almost thin air, sneaking underneath the bleachers to see Alice in her heartbroken state. "Hey, Alice," Hal started off, reaching forward in an attempt to comfort her.

Reeling back like she'd been touched by a vermin, Alice snapped at him, "Don't touch me, Hal!" Her voice was shaky but firm.

Hal reeled his arm back and watched her.

"What did you tell everyone at school about us?!" Alice demanded in a shaky firm tone. "And don't you dare lie to me, I saw the stares I've been getting all day!" She stared straight into his eyes.

"What?" Hal scoffed in disbelief. "You really think I'd go kissing and telling about us? They're probably guessing you're the one responsible for the prank at the Halloween house party since you didn't show up and a few other students saw you buying a ton of stuff at the costume store the other day." He shrugged coyly.

Alice suddenly went mute as it dawned on her that Hal might be right. No one at school knew she had been admitted to the psych ward for a few weeks so it was only right for them to think she was responsible for the Halloween house horror.

Hal let out a soft sigh as he moved closer to Alice and touched her shoulder. This time she didn't jump back. "And I'm sorry about the other day at your house, okay? Let's just put that past us, hmm," he trailed off in a mild whisper.

Alice found herself nodding softly in agreement as he gently wiped off her tears. She instantly began to think of how ridiculous it had been to blame Hal over the stares at school.

Gently getting up, Hal stretched out an arm towards Alice with a smile on his face. "C'mon, let's go," he yipped emphatically.

Clearing her shaky voice as she glanced up at his towering frame, Alice asked. "Where?"

"Wherever we decide! We're skipping school today," Hal stated emphatically with a tone of finality as he helped Alice up.

Alice had never flunked school and knew she'd get in trouble skipping school with Hal but she didn't mind as long as she got to spend quality time with him. It was just what she needed.

AFTER SKIPPING SCHOOL WITH HAL, Alice spent the entire day with him. In a clever plot to make her stay longer, Hal had proposed a date of any kind, right away. "But neither of us is even dressed for a date." Alice giggled hard at Hal's suggestion.

"The best things in life are spontaneous, my dear!" Hal chimed his reply with glee as he grabbed Alice by her hand and led her into the streets once it was almost dark out. A few minutes later, they arrived at a graveyard with decrepit headstones dotted across the length and breath of the land as it lay eerily silent.

"Oh, Hal. Seriously? A cemetery?" Alice scoffed in near disbelief but visible admiration at him as he led her towards an untouched patch of green earth in a distant corner of the cemetery and they both settled down on a tablecloth he spread out.

"What? Don't you like it?" Hal smirked at Alice with searching eyes.

Casually scanning around the silent rows and columns of headstones, cenotaphs and mini tombs, Alice returned her gaze to him. "It's gnarly," she quipped, "and sweet..." she trailed off in a giggle as she leaned in to kiss Hal on the lips. She noticed him blush for the first time and the butterflies in her stomach fluttered with excitement.

Hal pulled out a bottle of wine from his jacket— another surprise for Alice as well. Sitting opposite each other on the spread out tablecloth, they both began to take swigs of the wine bottle, passing it between themselves as they talked about anything and everything. Alice couldn't help but fall more in love with Hal as the romantic date was just what she needed. A few minutes into the date and she had even forgotten they were at a graveyard filled with nothing less than a million cadavers beneath the Earth.

"Imagine if one of these guys would pop out with thriller moves. That'll be a sight!" Hal randomly blurted after a swig of the bottle. Alice's eyes flew wide at his suggestion and Hal couldn't help but erupt into a hearty laughter. "Ha! You should see your face. I bet you'd take off running if it happens."

"Well, no fucking shit, Sherlock." Alice scoffed with an eye roll at Hal's weak attempt at scaring her. For a split second it almost felt like he got his kick from seeing her being scared shitless. She flashed him a smirk regardless as she shook any would-be thoughts from her head in order to focus on Hal's face that had contorted into a faint frown now.

Reaching for his backpack, Hal pulled out the Ouija board, placing it in between himself and Alice.

The sight of the damn board made Alice start to hyperventilate softly right away as she felt the board was what set off the last chain of catastrophic events in her life. Her stomach tightened in knots and she felt a sick feeling deep down as she glanced up at Hal. "Maybe we shouldn't," Alice casually echoed into the night, causing Hal to cast a startled gaze at her.

"What do you mean we shouldn't?" Hal piped up rhetorically with furrowed brows. "This is the best time to communicate with your dead sister. Especially now, when you're happy. She'll be happy as well," he rambled off in a futile effort.

Taking offense at the mention of her sister, Alice sprang up from the ground and yelled at Hal, "I SAID NO!"

A tentative silence ensued before Hal scrambled up to his feet to face Alice. "What's with the attitude? I'm just trying to show you how to contact me," he stated blatantly without batting an eye.

Alice couldn't believe what she was hearing. Hal still had plans of offing himself and from the sounds of it, he wanted her in on it. Taking a step back, Alice shook her head in disapproval. "Contact you? What are you, some twelve year old kid stuck in a jumanji box?!" she furiously snapped at him with bile seething up within her. She paused to catch her breath, cupped her palms over her face then let out a soft exhale as she put her arms down. "I'm sorry, Hal, but I can't do this anymore." She dropped the bombshell that made Hal blink rapidly like he had problems with his sight. "I mean, I barely know you and since you came into my life it's been one catastrophe after the other. Look, I know my life was already messed up without you in it, but I can't be with someone who makes it worse for me." She sighed dejectedly with a casual brush of her palm against her hair.

Hal remained transfixed to a spot like he was the one to see a ghost now. "You don't mean all of that now, do you?" he muttered.

Taking a few steps forward so she was close to him, Alice sneered at his face. "Read my lips, Hal, we're done!" With that, she spun around and stormed out of the graveyard alone, not minding the eerie chilly atmosphere and flickering fright within herself.

A few minutes later, she arrived home and unsurprisingly, this time she wasn't heartbroken or shaking like before. She was simply done. Needing someone to talk to, she decided to sneak into her brother's room first. Slipping into his room, Alice noticed he was fast asleep. There and then she realized how foolish her endeavors to speak with her dead sister were. Her brother probably needed her but she was too busy running around with Hal to even recall she had a brother most times. Feeling sorry for her actions, Alice slipped into her brother's bed and held him gently.

Stirring awake with a slurred grunt, Ethan sleepily noticed his sister was in his room. "You're back from the shaman today?" he muttered drowsily in his sleepy state.

Staring into nothingness as she cradled her brother, Alice replied stoically. "He's mad, Ethan," she whispered emphatically. "Mad as a hatter!"

CHAPTER

SIXTEEN

hy aren't you picking up?!
Pickup we need to talk!
You know I see you on your phone all day right? Pick up
and answer me!
You just might make me off myself already. Pick up!
Alice groaned to herself as she stared at the slew of text popping off in her cell phone every few minutes from a desperate Hal. Ever since she broke up with him, he'd gone bonkers with the texting and calling. He kept sending slews of unsolicited messages and demanding for Alice to reply to him. At dinner, despite her cell phone being on silent mode, Alice couldn't help but stare occasionally at the slew of texts from Hal, as they endlessly popped into her phone.

I see you having dinner with your family. Strange how I thought I was family as well. Alice's head jerked up from her plate and hidden cell phone as she cast a panicked glance around the curtains and caught sight of Hal's beady eyes peering into one of the windows. He hastily slithered into the darkness once their eyes met and Alice began to hyperventilate from fright. A lot of things were starting to not add up concerning Hal and she was getting concerned.

"Honey, are you alright?" Alice's mom reached out to hold her hand from across the table, noticing how they visibly trembled.

Her father and brother's attention were also drawn to her as she looked clearly shaken and on edge.

Knowing she couldn't continue keeping this secret from her parents, Alice wiped off apprehensive beads of sweat from her forehead as she announced. "I think I'm being stalked by a boy!" Her statement put her parents on edge as well as they moved to the edge of their seats, immediately wondering who this boy was.

"Oh my goodness, honey, I'm so sorry. Who's this boy?" Alice's mom asked carefully while her father listened on with watchful eyes.

"Hal. The new kid at school. I mean we hung out a couple of times as friends but after a while he began acting strange and I told him I couldn't do it anymore." Alice didn't hold back as she confessed it all to her parents even including the reason for the night when she'd come in visibly distraught and lied to her parents. She went on to confess to them about the Ouija board and the strange connection with Jane's spirit. Everyone listened attentively and exchanged glances in astonishment.

"Why didn't you say something earlier, hon," Alice's father asked calmly after she was done telling them everything that had brought her and Hal together. "You could have told us about him and I would have reported him to his father," he added with a tone of familiarity.

"Wait, what?" Alice blurted out at her father in confusion. "You know his dad?"

Looking rather perplexed, her father continued, "Sure, I do!"

Alice felt a nasty knot churn in the pit of her stomach.

"I work with his dad. We're good buddies. In fact, let me call him." Her father reached for his cellphone in his pocket and began scrolling through his contacts list.

Seeing everything from a whole different perspective now, a befuddled Alice slowly slunk away from the dining table and made a beeline for her room. She shut herself in as her mind was troubled by a whirlwind of thoughts as to who exactly Hal was.

Was the ouija board stuff all fake? Was I not really talking to my sister? She began to second guess everything that had happened so far as she was confused about what was real and what was not. Alice soon realized that the more she thought about everything, the deeper it started to hurt as she felt her entire foray with Hal had been a complete lie. She wondered if he deliberately baited her into the situation, just to hurt her in the end like everyone else.

Feeling claustrophobic as she lay sobbing on her bed, Alice slipped out into the yard and sat crying by herself. She didn't know what to think anymore, and truthfully, she might as well be done at this point. Suddenly, the dim street lights cast a long shadow in front of a sobbing Alice as Hal walked across the street and paused a few feet from her.

Slowly lifting her reddened face and puffy eyes from her knees, Alice stared up at Hal and surprisingly felt sorry for not trusting him enough. She knew he'd been so kind to her but her damaged heart always feared he might have an ulterior motive. She didn't want to believe it, but what was true anymore. Now, he just stood right there in front of her, watching her sob in silence.

"My dad is calling your dad," Alice sniffled a tense whisper. She then glanced up at Hal's expressionless eyes. "Let's get out of here, okay? I want to apologize." She sprang up and led the way this time, pulling Hal by his arm and leading the way into the dark evening.

"It's alright, I've got you." Hal held Alice's arm with a firm but soft grip as he gently tugged her to follow him. Despite feeling conflicted about Hal and everything in her life now, Alice felt she should give him one more chance. Deep down, she felt she knew better but at the same time she felt a sense of obligation towards Hal. He'd helped her consult with her dead sister's spirit, this was the least she could do for him. Moreover the last thing she wanted was to make him feel unappreciated as she knew that would hurt him. He'd been nothing but kind to her so far, right? Why was she afraid of him now?

What can it hurt? I'm sure my dad will be here to punish me soon anyways. She let go of every inhibition and followed Hal closely behind, down the trail by her house. Only this time, Hal began taking a series of twists and turns down the familiar path into quite unfamiliar terrain, casually crossing through closed off places in the woods like he had the entire map of the area in the palm of his hands.

Alice carefully and briskly followed suit, not wanting to miss a beat as Hal seemed really focused on his journey, consistently glancing around to make sure they didn't have company. She subtly wondered how long he'd been around these parts to know this many shortcuts but chose to keep silent as she walked behind him to wherever he was leading them to.

Glancing back, Alice noticed they were far off into the woods now and she could barely recognize which part of the woods they were in as everything seemed to look the same. The towering mahogany and pine trees sprawled up into the dark night sky while she could clearly hear critters scurry around the underlying bushes of the woods as they trudged on.

A flock of bats fluttered in the night sky out of some nearby cave and Alice barely even twitched as they all scurried close to her path, their cacophonous screeching audible in her ear as they whooshed past. She would normally be scared if she was by herself, but Hal was here and there was really no reason for her to be afraid as he also didn't flinch an eyelid to the swarming bats.

"I'm so sorry about everything," Hal muttered without glancing back as he led the way deeper into the woods once an eerie silence resumed.

Alice didn't reply immediately as she silently walked behind him with a barrage of thoughts plaguing her mind.

"It's just," Hal slurred like he was thinking of what to say, "falling in love with you was just a bonus. I never really saw that coming." He let out a sigh as he glanced back at Alice who didn't return his gaze as she deliberately stared down at her path and not his face.

Hal continued to lead the way once he noticed Alice wasn't

budging to his subtle pleas. "I mean, you were just a lonely girl at school. Of course I had to become friends with you," Hal rambled on. "I knew I wanted to be friends right from the very first day I set my eyes on you. I mean why else would I single you out like I did?" He let out a mild chuckle.

Alice didn't find anything funny by the slightest bit. Matter of fact, she was totally repulsed by Hal's remark that if she'd known her way back to the trail that led home, she would have turned back right away. Her brows narrowed in anger as she fought within herself to steady her hyperventilating breaths. "So I was your fucking pity project, huh?" she blurted out to stop Hal dead in his tracks.

Turning back to cast a glance at her, Hal retorted in a mild stutter. "Wait, what? That's what you think? C'mon!" He groaned as he tried tugging gently on Alice's arm but she roughly yanked her arm away from his.

"That's what I know!" Alice quipped once she flung her arm away from Hal's. She noticed how gobsmacked and embarrassed he looked at her reaction.

"Oh my goodness, Alice, you really do not have to be this dramatic! I already apologized so what else do you expect from me?!" Hal piped up in a self righteous stance as Alice took a few steps back away from him.

Fighting back the tears welling up in her eyes, Alice shook her head. "That's the problem, Hal. You're dangerous and toxic for me. You keep saying you're sorry but keep doing things to hurt me. You never care to listen to me and always want things done your way. I just can't." She broke off and sobbed softly, taking a step back from him.

Moving closer to her, Hal replied in a firm tone. "What do you mean I never listen? At least I helped you talk to your sister, that should count for something right?"

Alice immediately felt her stomach churn in knots at Hal's statement. She felt sick to her stomach that he wanted to use the Ouija board as leverage now and she regretted ever agreeing to that in the first place. "You asshole!" Alice gasped in near disbelief as her jaw tightened and so did a fist which she struggled to not slam it in Hal's face.

"Ok...I'm sorry, that came out wrong," Hal tried to redeem himself with another apology but Alice wasn't having it this time.

"No, screw you, asshole! How dare you bring my sister into this?!" Alice snapped back at him with a shaky voice and tears running down her red face. She felt utterly heartbroken that Hal would even say something like that.

Hal took a step forward and tried to grab Alice's arm in an attempt to plead with her but Alice swung her arm away, avoiding contact with him.

"Don't fucking touch me," she cried in a still that shaky voice as she doubled back to avoid him. "You're just like all of them. You just want to use me for your benefit then be on your merry way to god-fucking-knows-where," she stuttered amidst sobs.

"Alice, I said I'm sorry! Now come on, let's keep going!" Hal tried to snatch her flailing arm but Alice doubled back one more time and she let out a shriek of terror as her left heel clipped against a twig, tripping her into a hole behind and dragging her entire body along with her. Hal snatched her by the arm at the last minute but surprisingly couldn't save her from the fall as both of them tumbled into a ditch about fifteen feet in height, right in the middle of the woods. Alice passed out right away once she hit the hard earth in the empty hole. Hal, however, broke his fall gently and didn't pass out upon landing like Alice had.

CHAPTER

SEVENTEEN

"Owww...shhiittt!!!" Alice cussed in despair once she finally came to at the bottom of the pit she'd fallen into. Her head was ringing with a splitting migraine and her blurred vision was taking time to clear up as she squinted at the ripping pain ringing through her skull. For a split moment, she had no idea where she was or how she'd arrived there as she groggily pulled herself up in a sitting position in attempts to clear her head. Blinking her eyes steadily to acclimate to the dim environment, Alice noticed the hole was dark except for a lit candle which Hal sat beside with his knees folded up to his chin as he carefully watched her wake up.

"Hey, welcome back," Hal casually quipped to break the silence after a few minutes of Alice's soft grunting and glancing around.

"Where the hell are we?" Alice retorted in a tense tone as she glanced straight up at the sky and partial view of trees.

"We're in the rabbit hole," Hal casually announced to her, also looking up at the visible sky overhead. "We're underground. It's an old bunker of my dad's," he stated emphatically as he leaned against the walls of the pit then let out a heavy sigh. "Look, Alice, I need you to understand that I'm really sorry about everything, okay?" Hal resumed his apology which had brought them here in the first place. "I guess things just sort of happened too fast and I thought you were fine with it all. But it seems I was too hard on you. And I'm sorry for not listening to you."

Hal's apology sounded heartfelt to a listening third party but not to Alice. She was well aware of his cunningly manipulative nature and knew just how sweet and charming he could be when trying to get his way with her. Deep down in her mind she promised herself to never be the vulnerable girl who craved attention again but she knew she had to get out of this hole first.

"Are you listening to me at all?" Hal quipped to snap her from her short reverie as she had been mute all throughout the five minutes of his rewritten apology speech.

Nodding her head affirmatively, Alice muttered. "It's fine. It's fine. I forgive you, Hal," she tried avoiding eye contact with him as she hastily replied to him.

A tentative silence ensued and Alice was just about to ask a seemingly unbothered Hal how they were going to get out of the hole when he piped up, "I can feel your lies, Alice," Hal retorted in a cold tone, his eyes conveying his disappointment in Alice's futile attempt at trying to deceive him. "You can't paint white roses red and expect me not to see, Alice. Not possible." He shook his head with a rather devious smirk at Alice's ignorance.

Alice's heart skipped multiple beats as her stomach churned in multiple knots again. Hal was definitely not what she had thought him to be as he was looking more like a deranged person by the minute. She couldn't help but battle with the trepidation within herself that he was going to do something eerily dangerous to her since he didn't believe her. Watching his glassy cold eyes pierce into her soul gave her the shivers, and for the first time, Alice saw Hal for what he truly was; an unexplainable enigma of a human being that she shouldn't have gotten herself involved with in the first place. She wondered if he had any underlying mental health issues but knew better than to rile him up completely with any questions of such.

Alice??? Alice!!! Alice, where are you??? Faint voices filtered into the hole from above as it sounded like a search party had been sent out after Alice. Her ears perked up in the hole and she sprang up from where she was seated with a glint of hope in her eyes.

"HELLLPPPP!!!!" Alice cried out at the top of her lungs as she yelled out into the opening above the hole.

Hal's face contorted in a sinister smirk as he watched a panicky Alice shuffle around the hole in futile attempts to get noticed by whoever was out looking for her. She would move from side to side then wave her arms flagrantly; almost like she was intent on flagging down a plane with her bare hands.

Her hair was tousled and filled with dirt from the fall but she didn't care as all she wanted was to get out of the hole and far away from the psychotic Hal.

"SOMEBODY HELP ME, I'M DOWN HERE!!!" Alice's loud voice quivered in her throat as she cried out in a louder voice, now scared that no one was coming to her rescue. She wiped off the streaking hot tears from her red cheeks as she yelled out again in sobs. "PLE-ASSEE...GET ME OUT OF HERE!!!" She kept crying out but was greeted with an eerie silence while Hal hissed through his teeth and shook his head.

"Save your strength, honey, it's useless calling out when no one's gonna hear you." Hal cackled sardonically at Alice but she defiantly kept screaming out for help, promoting his cackling to grow louder along with her voice.

Once Alice couldn't keep up with the screaming and yelling, she crumbled back down on the ground and curled up in a fetal position as she began to cry her eyes out.

Hal, who had been having a good laugh at her yelling, surprisingly moved close to her then lay behind her, throwing his arm around her body and pulling her close to himself as he whispered in her ear, "Shhhh...it's okay, my love. It's okay." He kept muttering softly into her ear as she sobbed in his arms. "I promise everything will get better, my love." He planted a gentle kiss on her head and more tears sluiced down Alice's cheeks as she had no option but to lay in Hal's arms, crying and sobbing softly at her unfortunate stroke of luck in making friends or even having a boyfriend.

STILL LAYING ALMOST motionless in the fetal position on the patched earth beneath her, Alice listened as the loud calls for her name began to slowly drown off in the distance, causing her to whimper to herself with a red face and nibbling her anxiety out on her fingernails. Whoever was out there looking for her was long gone and she was left alone with the mad hatter in the hole. Hal still held onto her as the drowning calls finally silenced and the sounds that replaced them were chittering night critters along with Alice's non-stop sobbing.

Hal was somewhat repulsed by how much Alice was crying as she did look like a heartbroken mess now that she didn't stop. Regardless, his amorous affection for her made him pull her closer and whisper into her ear with a soft but firm tone, "Don't worry, you're safe with me." He kissed her on the cheek and a sudden eerie silence enveloped the pit and Alice was just done crying as her puffy red eyes couldn't go on anymore.

She just stared up at the length of the hastily dug hole sprawling up into the night sky splattered with stars. There was no moon tonight; making everything more scary for Alice as she had to really squint hard to find her way around the hole she'd dropped in. Hal, however, looked like he did just fine in the dark, snatching whatever he wanted out of thin air at will as he reached for his backpack that had spilled out due to the drop.

Alice's meandering mind wandered to her parents and how they must be panicking due to her sudden absence. She guessed they were the ones out searching for her and wondered if she had been declared missing after revealing Hal's strange identity and demeanor. She nudged her elbow backwards a bit, poking him to alertness as she picked her head up in an attempt to glance back at him with her bloodshot eyes. "You should go back before your dad worries about you," Alice muttered randomly, slightly surprising Hal as he never expected her to care about him—especially not now. Perhaps she was scared to her wits of him and wanted him gone.

Letting off a random scoff, Hal replied blatantly, "He won't!"

"But my dad was just calling him before we left." Alice reiterated emphatically in a soft tone.

"We have different families!" Hal snapped back with a tone of finality like he was done discussing the subject. A tentative moment of awkward and eerie silence enveloped the hole again and Alice could clearly hear an owl hoot high up in a tree, right over the pit.

Turning over to face Hal squarely, Alice gently cupped his slender but jagged jaw as she stared into his eyes amorously; unsure of what she was feeling inside of her but wanting to fix her relationship with him for some reason. She stared into his eyes and noticed tears of anguish behind them. For a split second, under the cover of darkness, he looked way older than he claimed to be and Alice wondered what exactly his story was. She hoped he would eventually confide in her someday to tell her everything. "I am sorry your family sucks, okay?" Alice pleaded rhetorically with Hal as she gently grazed her thumb against his cheek then reached up to flick some stray strands of hair away from his forehead. She wiped her eyes and let out a soft sigh. "I am so so sorry. You deserved better," she quipped softly, still staring into his sullen eyes that couldn't hide his faint surprise at her sudden change in reaction.

Hal's demeanor swiftly switched from surprise to melted affection as he pulled Alice so close to him their bodies pressed into each other as they lay on the ground. "You do too, Alice!" Hal piped up emphatically, his emotions rife in both gleaming eyeballs. "You deserve me. We deserve each other," he reiterated with a mild scoff as he gently caressed Alice's flailing ponytail behind her back.

Alice just stared back stoically at Hal after his response. She felt like she had to reply to him but just couldn't bring her lips to move anymore. Instead she felt a fuzzy lightheaded feeling hit her as she swore she was flickering in and out. Or maybe it was just the limited supply of oxygen in the hole that was starting to affect her. Whatever it was, it made Alice casually turn her back to Hal and pass out in a not-so-peaceful sleep marred by repetitive nightmares.

After what felt like an hour or two, Alice blinked awake, this time without the groan of a migraine as she felt slightly better than before. She tried to poke her elbows back and hit nothing but wind which made her scramble to sit up in a flash. Glancing around the hole, Alice realized she was all alone and Hal was nowhere in sight. Recalling her girls scout camp days, Alice began to carefully scale up the sides of the pit, groaning and shrieking as patches of red earth crumbled from the sides and rained on her with each advance upwards. The expanding sight of the hole above her was the only flicker of hope she had to hold onto as she struggled through the climb, her shoulders and knees aching badly.

After what felt like forever and a half, Alice finally made it out of the hole. She staggered face flat on the ground and let out a loud gasp as she rolled over then inhaled and exhaled fresh air after hours down in the hole. She glanced around the surrounding trees in slight panic, hoping Hal wasn't somewhere waiting for her to come out. She seemed to be able to think clearly again and didn't want to see Hal again. She wondered how he'd left her there all alone after everything he'd said but was glad he eventually left her alone. Surprisingly, the moon was out in its full glory and it had actually helped Alice illuminate her way out of the hole. Once she finally caught her wind, Alice rolled over, got up on her feet and began to do a zombie-like dash through the woods, as fast as her aching legs could carry her while she whimpered and sobbed along the way.

Cupping her palm on her mouth was the only way Alice could

stop herself from bawling out in tears as she eased through the woods on her way home. The fear of Hal lurking somewhere in the shadows was enough to keep her quiet as she hurried through the endless twists of narrow trails, trying to locate the familiar paths that led back home.

Her heart raced a thousand beats per second as she constantly cast nervous glances behind her shoulder, expecting Hal to emerge out of the shadows anytime soon. Alice's knees were almost giving out, prompting her to stumble and stagger through the trail as she went. She had to lean against the hard barks of trees for support multiple times while also quickly catching stop breaks. She moved as fast as she could manage, her mind a train wreck of all the things Hal had said and how different his actions were.

"He's a fucking psychopath! That's what he is." Alice sniffled in soft sobs as she hurried through the woods. Once she caught sight of her house rearing up in the distance as she waded into the neighborhood, Alice let go of any inhibitions she had and screamed at the top of her lungs. "SOMEBODY HELP! PLEASE. I NEED HELP!!!" Alice cried out in an erratic cry-yell that attracted much attention. A few neighbors peeped out their window and when they saw the familiar figure of Alice limping through the streets, they dashed out to help the traumatized girl.

"Alice! Are you alright?" An elderly couple who lived close by called out to Alice as she limped through the streets with tears in her eyes and her dirty outfit. Alice could barely give them a reply as she kept snuggling and limping on her way.

"HELPPP!!!" Alice cried out in almost robotic fashion as she just couldn't stop herself from shaking.

The elderly woman hurried from her front porch into the street and blocked Alice's path. More neighbors had begun pouring out of their houses to see what all the ruckus was about. "Tell me what happened, honey." The elderly woman gently cupped Alice's face with both hands.

"He hurt me!" Alice broke down in more quivering sobs.

The woman swung around and yelled at her husband. "Call 911 now!" Turning back to face Alice, she held her tightly and whispered softly. "You'll be fine, Alice. You're a good girl. You'll be fine."

Just then, Alice noticed the lights in her house come on as her mother and father bolted out the door, racing towards her with fright in their eyes.

CHAPTER

EIGHTEEN

The police arrived and asked if they could take Alice in for a brief questioning. Her parents accompanied her to the precinct, adamant that they won't let their daughter be questioned alone. The police chief eventually gave in and let the family huddle together beside Alice in the interrogation room. "Okay, Alice, this is gonna be real quick. We just need you to help us identify this Hal person. It appears someone of similar interest happens to be on our radar."

Alice's parents exchanged knowing glances before glancing back at their silent daughter with expectant eyes.

"Before that, I'd like to specifically ask you where you were last night when you went missing." The police chief clasped both palms together as he fixed his attention on Alice.

Despite all she'd been through this evening, Alice was still torn between telling the truth and lying to protect Hal from harm. There was something that was drawing her to him still, though she was scared of him at the same time. Her indecisiveness was written clearly on her face as she stared down at the empty desk in deep contemplation.

"Are you safe," the police chief suddenly questioned to snap Alice's attention back to full alertness. "Is it Hal? Did he threaten you in any kind? We can't help you if we don't know what happened and who Hal is." He blurted out a slew of questions before pausing. When Alice still didn't answer, he let out a sigh of frustration. "We just want to help you feel safe again, Alice."

Reaching for her daughter's arm, Alice's mother gently squeezed it and leaned in to whisper. "It's alright, honey. Tell the policeman everything." She cooed in a reassuring tone that made Alice feel a bit safe for the first time that evening.

Clearing her throat to pull the attention to herself, Alice glanced up to meet the police chief's gaze then quipped. "I was in a rabbit hole with him tonight. He pushed me down there when we had a little misunderstanding."

"That fucker, I'll kill him!" Alice's dad cussed out with clenched fists and jaw. The chief signaled him to not say anything that might make her stop talking and he went silent again, seething in fury.

Alice told them everything, from how she'd met Hal at school to their eerie escapades with the Ouija board and spirits of their dead siblings. Alice's parents couldn't believe what they were hearing and neither did the police chief, but they all kept mute to allow her to finish. "...and that was how I climbed out of the hole and ran home," She muttered softly in conclusion as she wrapped up the mind boggling tale of her friendship with Hal.

Alice's mom grabbed her tightly and sobbed in fright. "Oh my god, honey! I am so sorry. After this, you are right, my sweet bat, we need to remember your sister."

"Hold on just a second," the police chief broke the silence after Alice's story as he got up from his seat then walked towards the door, signaling an unseen figure to step in. Another officer came in with a scrawny lanky teenager that looked nothing like Hal. "Is this who you were hanging out with tonight, Alice," the chief asked slowly in a firm tone.

Alice stared in disbelief at the equally nervous boy that had been brought in. He looked or acted nothing like Hal and she couldn't even recall running into him at school.

"No, no, I'm afraid that's not him." Alice shook her head in disapproval after staring the teenager up and down.

Letting out a defeated sigh, the police chief signaled the officer to take the boy out before he returned to his seat, all eyes trailed on his movements. "I'm afraid that's the only Hal in this town, Alice," he informed them, which stunned Alice and her parents. "I'll be bringing in a sketch artist so your daughter can describe the boy and hopefully we can start from there." With that, the police chief got up and exited the interrogation room, leaving behind the distraught and discombobulated family.

"That's not Hal. Hal's real though, I didn't imagine him. Maybe he gave me a wrong name, but that's the name he used at school, too," Alice whispered in disbelief as her parents comforted her.

ALICE'S PARENTS were instructed to leave the interrogation room once the sketch artist arrived to take a sketch of Alice's mysterious boyfriend.

"How dark were his eyes, honey," the female sketch artist asked Alice with a sweet smile as she kept sketching all over the paper each time she asked Alice a question.

"Uhm, he has really dim eyes and a firm jaw like this..." she gestured with her hands just how Hal's face was structured and the sketch artist carried on.

"Any other things you can remember," the sketch artist asked after the sketch of Hal had taken form.

"Oh and he makes hats!" Alice piped up emphatically but the sketch artist had a demeanor that said that piece of information wasn't really going to help them now. "Lots of hats. I call him the mad hatter," she muttered softly as she trailed off.

The sketch artist observed Alice for a bit and then scribbled on her sketch pad. "Alright then. Mad hatter, got it," she chimed as she got up. "I'll be back shortly." She flashed a reassuring smile at Alice then trudged out of the interrogation room.

Approximately thirty minutes passed before the police chief walked back into the interrogation room with the sketch artist closely following behind. "I'm afraid, Alice, that it appears that no other person by the name of Hal lives in this town. Other than that scrawny kid we just brought in here."

He shrugged his burly shoulders in slight defeat as he just couldn't comprehend what was going on in Alice's life. She seemed way too troubled for a teen and he was of the silent opinion that her parents had taken her out of the psych ward a bit too early.

"That's impossible!" Alice's shaky voice roared back at the police chief as her limbs began palpitating from severe anxiety coursing through her veins. At this point, Alice was just done with everything as she couldn't tell if she was starting to lose her mind or not. She wasn't sure of what was real and what wasn't as everything just seemed to be one scrambled mess of vivid experiences.

Tears slid freely down her cheeks at her realization that this was another dead end and she felt a bitter knot churn in the pit of her stomach. Placing her head on the desk before her, Alice broke down in soft sobs and whimpering as she felt no one believed her. Their eyes all said she was batshit crazy, albeit no one dared to say it out— not even her mother standing outside and looking in through the plexiglass.

The police chief let out a sigh as he watched Alice breakdown in tears. He knew she wouldn't be able to answer any further questions and signaled the sketch artist to go fetch the precinct therapist.

A few minutes later, a lady smartly dressed in a suit with reading glasses walked into the interrogation room and sat beside Alice. Despite not knowing Alice, the therapist started off by comforting the heartbroken teenager, gently cradling her shoulder and whispering softly in her ear. "It's fine if they don't believe you. I do."

Alice's head perked up from the desk at the therapist's statement, casting her reddened eyes at the lady.

"I don't know what's," Alice's voice quivered and hiccuped as she tried to explain herself teary eyed to the sweet smiling therapist.

"Shhhh," the therapist hushed Alice almost immediately. "You don't have to say anything else. We can always talk about this some time when you're feeling up to it, alright?" The therapist smiled another sweet smile at Alice and the latter tried to stop her sniffling, sobbing and whimpering.

"WHAT HAS HAPPENED to your daughter is a very strange phenomenon I must say," the police chief stated to Alice's parents from outside the room as they watched Alice and the therapist through the window.

They silently glanced at him then back at their daughter. They couldn't blame the man really as what was going on with Alice had now put them on edge more than Jane's incident. Deep down, the couple greatly dreaded the misfortune of losing another child and were determined to do all within their power to save Alice.

"She'll return home with both of you while I'll be charging my men with finding this so-called bunker she talks about," the police chief announced to Alice's listening parents as they watched the therapist work with Alice.

Turning to face the police chief, Alice's father had a confused crease in his brows as he stated emphatically, confident in what he was saying, "According to the old maps of this town, there definitely are some old bunkers laying around in the woods."

"You're correct," the police chief concurred with Alice's dad but countered him. "There were old bunkers in the area, but they've all been sealed off..."

"Then where did she fall?" Alice's dad shuffled closer to the chief with a tensed tone and concerned eyes. "I mean we could clearly see the dirt on her clothes when she came running out the woods." He let out another tensed sigh then rubbed his aching temple.

"That's exactly what we're going to find out," the police chief blurted out in a calm retort before starting down the length of the hallway. "My team will be canvassing the woods to try and figure out which bunker it was. Once we do, we'll be one step closer to figuring things out."

"Thank you, Sir. Are we allowed to take her home now," Alice's mom asked the chief.

"Yes, we can't get anything more from Alice tonight. Go home, get some rest, and hopefully we'll have more answers tomorrow."

Alice and her parents were sent home with a police escort which was assigned to keep watch over her house for the time being. Although it wasn't much, the idea that Hal wouldn't come snooping around due to the police presence out front, was enough reason for Alice to at least catch some shut eye when she finally returned from the precinct. She desperately hoped they would catch the real Hal soon so everyone would stop looking at her like she was batshit crazy.

CHAPTER
NINETEEN

Alice was under the watchful eyes of everyone back home and her mother made sure she never left her sight even for a second. After dinner, Alice was sitting alone on a couch, staring stoically at the TV screen when her father silently took position beside her.

They both watched the broadcast of a music festival in silence for a bit before he turned to ask his daughter. "How do you feel? I mean genuinely. You don't have to lie to me." He flashed a smile at his daughter as he handed her a cup of her favorite frozen yogurt.

Alice couldn't help but at least mirror her father's smile as the frozen yogurt was enough bribe to get her talking. "Hmm, I feel like a trailer load of trash but I'm glad I'm home with you guys," she retorted with a smile of hers to ease the tension between her and her father.

Alice's father scoffed heartily at his daughter's mild joke which was a sign that she didn't hold anything against him. "Haha, that's funny, Al." He chortled softly then allowed a tentative silence to ensue before announcing in a soft tone, "I'm truly sorry for everything you've been through, Alice. I'm sorry for not being a perfect father figure to you and your siblings and I promise to do better starting from today, okay?" He reached gently for her arm and lightly placed his hand on her arm. "We're a family and should have each other's backs any time, any day. Believe we all got yours. We'll get through this together, hmm?"

Alice nodded affirmatively, albeit with a small reassuring smile on her face. "I know, Dad."

Just then, Alice's mom walked in on the heartfelt conversation between father and daughter. She was glad Alice was no longer talking crazy stuff about her father doing bad things to her dead sister as the sight of them smiling at each other was the most comforting thing she could experience now. "Your dad's right, Alice. We'll always have your back as a family. Okay?" She quipped lovingly at her daughter as she walked forward and bent over to gently caress Alice's hair.

For some reason, Alice felt overwhelmed by the show of affection from her parents and she sprang up to throw her arms around her mother's shoulder. "Thanks mom, thanks dad," she muttered softly to make her mother feel butterflies in her stomach.

Her dad also got up and embraced both of them in a more secured family hug, glancing behind himself as he did to urge Ethan to join them. Ethan reluctantly walked into the living room from the kitchen where he was watching. His father gently pulled him into the group hug as the entire family gathered round in a circle with arms around each other, for the first time in as long as they could remember.

The family reunion was broken off by the shrill ring of the front door bell as the police had arrived again with more details regarding their investigation. Alice's dad hurriedly answered the door and a detective assigned to the case strolled in after introducing himself and shaking hands with Alice's dad. He was ushered into the living room where the entire family waited in anticipation for any breakthrough news. "Well, we've got some good news and some bad news." The detective started off once he was seated.

"My family's had enough bad news. Spit out the good news first," Alice's dad hastily piped up as he sat beside his wife and daughter.

"We found the bunker your daughter crawled out of," the detective stated emphatically and Alice let out a sigh of relief and a small smile. Finally, something was starting to add up and people won't think she was making this whole thing up. "But it was empty and there were no traces of this mysterious Hal your daughter speaks of," the detective rambled on, subtly dropping the bad news that made Alice's face contort back in a frown.

Her mother gently caressed Alice's back as she noticed Alice's dissatisfaction at the news.

Opening up a file that was clasped underneath his armpit, the detective pulled out a sheet of paper with lots of names printed neatly on it before casually carrying on with the narrating of his findings. "Another peculiarity is that there's absolutely nothing in the school records that matches your daughter's description of this Hal person. Trust me, I had to read through yearbooks of almost a decade looking for this Hal character," he scoffed softly like he was almost in doubt of Alice's sanity.

Alice took offense at the detective as she sprang up and glanced around wide eyed at everyone. "Well other people at school must have seen him, right," she piped up rhetorically with a shaky tone.

The detective gently shook his head disapprovingly. "I'm sorry miss, but no one at your school seems to remember if they saw you with such a strange person or not."

"Then they're lying! Hal even beat one of them up for picking on me! He protected me from all the bullies at school!" *Of course they won't remember, they only notice me when they attack me. None of them even like me so they would lie about it either way!*

"It's okay, Alice, we'll find him." Alice's mom tried to placate her daughter.

Alice yanked her arm away from her mom as she wasn't having

any of it. She saw how everyone looked at her with pity and she hated it. She clenched her fists as a surge of anger ripped through her frame. Without saying anything, she stormed out of the living room and made a beeline for her room where she popped some of her medication that was from the psych ward as she needed to calm down before she might literally explode from her wildly thumping heart.

ALICE FINALLY AGREED to see a therapist as things weren't looking any better for her. Her mother was more than happy to drive her to the therapist and stayed behind waiting for her in the waiting room so that she'd feel more comfortable opening up to the therapist.

Seated on a sprawling couch in the therapist's office, Alice continuously shook her right leg as she waited for the therapist to start. Her borderline anxiety of opening up to people was getting the best of her but she knew she needed to do this for herself and her family. The therapist, a middle aged brunette woman with horn-rimmed reading glasses, sat across from Alice. "Nervous," she asked softly as she noticed Alice's twitching leg.

Still shaking her leg as she glanced stoically at the center rug in the room, Alice muttered in reply, "I don't know anymore. I don't know what to feel anymore. Or what's even real!"

"Well, that's perfectly understandable, Alice, but I believe we can both work to identify what is real and just what isn't, hmm?"

Slowly pulling up her gaze from the center carpet to level it with the therapist's gaze, Alice finally confessed what she'd been thinking all these while. "I feel like I'm going crazy," she blurted out with a straight face. "Everyone feels the same, too. They're just lying to make me feel like I'm not. Which even makes it fucking worse," Alice cussed out in anger as she clenched her fists and jaw, stifling a sob that was about to break out.

"Hey there, take it easy on yourself now, Alice," the therapist retorted, "we all have our individual perceptions of reality but that doesn't make mine any more or less authentic than yours, now does it?"

Alice actually thought about it for a split moment before nodding affirmatively in reply.

"Good!" The therapist beamed an emphatic bright smile. "Now, how about we work towards trying to differentiate between what is real and what's not. Care to try that with me?" She was always making sure to ask Alice's opinion and permission after every question or suggestion, thereby making her feel as though she was a part of the therapeutic process.

"That doesn't make sense! It won't work," Alice replied without batting an eyelid as she stared blankly at the therapist.

"C'mon, don't knock it until you try it, sweetheart." The therapist flashed another reassuring smile at Alice then reached into her jacket pocket to retrieve a renaissance styled stop clock with a chain attached.

Alice stared at the piece of jewelry with a frown of confusion as she watched the smiling therapist stretch it forward and hold it up.

"Now, is this clock in my hand real," the therapist asked in an almost enchanting tone as her hand remained still but the clock swung lazily from side to side as it dangled from its chain.

"Uhm, yeah," Alice raised an eyebrow as she replied with suspicion.

"Great start!" The therapist beamed a grin and then asked in the same enchanting voice, "Is this clock working or not?"

Alice slowly adjusted forward on her seat, squinting into the clock which had begun to swing faster on its axis, causing her eyeballs to consistently dart from side to side as she tried to see if the clock was really working. She caught an arm move and yelled out almost excitedly. "It works!"

"Excellent," the therapist calmly replied as the clock still kept swinging in her grasp. "So now we've established that you can figure out what is real. We just have to work on the nether realm spilling into your three dimensional view," the therapist casually rambled on like she hadn't just said something utterly ridiculous and almost impossible.

How was it possible for a human to see spirits? Was the therapist a spirit as well? These were the random thoughts coursing through Alice's mind as she watched the click swing from side to side, making her slightly dizzy. *Well, that was what Hal had to be since everyone was claiming to have no knowledge of him.*

"Excuse me, what?" Alice shook her head as she snapped out from the hypnosis she was already drowning in.

Beaming another reassuring smile, the therapist calmly replied, "Don't worry your pretty head. Keep your eyes on the clock and you'll do just fine." She urged Alice to keep staring at the swinging clock and Alice did just that without much resistance. Once she noticed Alice's attention was fully wrapped in the swinging clock again, the therapist stoically echoed, "Everything you see here must be real. If not, it is a deeply intricate delusion. Say it!"

Like a programmed robot, Alice rambled on after the therapist with her eyes fixated on the swinging clock. "Everything I see here must be real. If not, it is a deeply intricate delusion." Alice was made to repeat this over and over again as the therapist told her to make the quote her waking mantra. Alice agreed and was finally set free from the nauseating hypnotism.

The session was wrapped up in earnest and Alice was led out of the room to meet her mom in the waiting room, who was on the phone. "Maybe we need to move to another town so that our children can heal? Oh, Alice is done, we'll talk more tonight, hun. See you soon!"

Alice's mom hung up the phone and sprang up at the sight of Alice and hurried towards her. She grabbed her gently by her shoulders and gazed into her eyes. "Hey honey, are you okay," she asked and Alice just nodded silently. "Your dad and I have been thinking, maybe it's time we move out of this town and move someplace else.

Hmm, what do you think, are you down to move?" Alice's mom asked carefully.

"Well, I think a move right now could cause more trauma to Alice, or it could just be the healing your daughter needs, it would be hard to say," the therapist echoed from behind and everyone glanced at her and then back at Alice with expectant eyes.

Alice took a deep breath then softly replied, "I wanna leave."

CHAPTER

TWENTY

A lice sat on the edge of her bed in her room, taking in what would be the final sights and sounds of where she'd spent much of her life. She felt a flood of nostalgia envelop her as she recalled how she and her siblings had all grown up in this neighborhood as one big, happy family. A faint smile formed on Alice's face as she recalled riding her bike through the paved streets when she was much younger.

Everything had been so much simpler then and she wished she could turn back the hands of time. Unfortunately, the recent events had put a sour taste in her mouth and Alice wanted more than anything now to leave the town. She knew she wasn't going to miss anyone, or any activities, as she had already lost any hope of making friends here. Especially after Hal.

A chill shiver ran up Alice's spine at the thought of Hal. She wondered where he was and if he still lurked in the shadows watching her like before. She'd checked the windows numerous times after having a feeling of being watched but saw nothing. Even if Hal did somehow sneak around to watch her, he did it carefully due to the presence of the police patrol car that was still parked out front.

Alice tucked her flailing blonde hair behind her ears as she let out a deep sigh. Her mind was a marauding mess of thoughts as all she could think of was that rabbit hole and the ghosts that haunted her dreams. She wondered where fake-Hal had spawned from and if she would have ended up worse if she had still been with him. "Okay, stop thinking about him, stop thinking about him!" Alice sighed to herself as she tried to shake away the thoughts of Hal from her mind.

Trudging across the length of her room, Alice paused at her sister's box of clothes and began fishing out the items she wanted from the box, tossing them on the bed as she chose them. Once she was done, she switched her shirt and wore one of her sister's punk themed tee shirts. Staring at herself in the mirror, Alice realized how much she'd become a shadow of herself. Her eyes were sunken and dark from crying so much and her cheekbones were jutted. Alice scoffed at her facial appearance before a faint smirk creased on her cheeks as she recalled a hilarious incident that had happened whilst Jane had this exact shirt on.

Jane had attended a Kid Rock concert and ended up getting a tattoo on her left buttcheek after getting hammered and despite Alice's plea to not do it. Jane had woken up in a frenzied craze the next morning upon sighting the tattoo, screaming up a storm at Alice for not stopping her. All Alice could do was laugh her eyes out at her sister and even now that she thought about the incident, she couldn't help but chortle out in mild bursts of laughter.

Faintly shaking her head at the memory filling her with happy thoughts, Alice resumed picking and choosing from her sister's box when a knock echoed on her door.

Ethan walked in with a sullen expression on his face. He took one look around and noticed Alice had already begun packing. "Mom and dad say we're moving," he blurted out once he stepped into the room, shutting the door behind him, and leaned against it.

Alice took a deep breath to steady herself and nodded affirmatively. "Yes, Ethan. We're moving," she replied and watched her brother take a few steps towards her.

"Well, I say it's about fucking time!" Ethan scoffed and Alice felt relieved that she wouldn't have to feel bad about making the decision.

"Aren't you going to pack your stuff as well?" Alice asked her brother as she carried on with the packing, moving clothes from a bigger box to a medium sized one and tossing out the hangers.

"Trust me, Alice, if I could walk out of here without so much as a hairpin, I'd be fine with that. This place is fucking jinxed! I can't wait to get the hell out of here, too!" Ethan emphatically retorted as he settled at the edge of his sister's bed and watched her pack.

"Oh, that's true! Well, how about school? Won't you miss anyone? Friends? Girlfriend, maybe?" Alice found herself more concerned about her brother and how he was taking the news of their relocation. Deep down she hoped she wasn't turning his life upside down and she promised herself that if she were to notice the slightest bit of hesitation from him, she might reconsider the decision to move.

Shrugging his shoulders, Ethan responded with a scoff. "School?" he questioned in disbelief. "School sucks and so does everyone in it. You know that Al." He casually waved off her question.

A tentative silence elapsed between both siblings as Alice realized she and Ethan had more in common than she knew. Or at least they were starting to.

Ethan was the polar opposite of Alice at school as he had his group of friends and was a regular starter on the school's football team. Regardless it seemed he had always felt left out and the death of his sister exacerbated his anxiety, causing him to be slightly reclusive around people as he'd heard so many stories concerning his sister's death. One such story even postulated that his sister was pregnant and couldn't live with the shame which was why she killed herself.

"School sucks!" Ethan echoed softly to break the silence.

Alice was about to say something else when her room door suddenly flung open and her mother rushed inside with eyes frighteningly wide open. "They found him!" Alice's mom announced to their hearing with short breaths.

"Found who?" Alice had a confused expression on her face.

"Hal...well the guy who claimed to be Hal. C'mon! We've got to head to the station right now." Her mother hurried back out of the room. Alice exchanged a silent glance with her brother before dashing out of the room after her mother.

ALICE'S HEART was audibly thumping against her ribcage as she nibbled nervously on her fingernails and shook her right leg endlessly while waiting in the police chief's office with her mother. Noticing her daughter's demeanor riddled with anxiety, Alice's mom reached over and gently cradled her shoulder, pulling her close for a gentle side hug. "Don't be sacred honey, it'll all be over soon." She planted a soft kiss on Alice's head and Alice tried to feign a faint smile as she pulled her face up to her mothers.

"Thanks, Mom," Alice muttered and just then the door flung open and the burly police chief rushed in with a sense of urgency, clasping a file beneath his armpit. Both mother and daughter slowly disengaged and properly adjusted in their seats as the police chief walked around to his seat at the other end of the table.

"Sorry for keeping you waiting, ladies. I just really need to make sure we all understand what or who we're dealing with here." The police chief settled into his seat, adjusted it forward, and then slapped the file before him on the table. Both Alice and her mom's gaze moved from the file up to the police chief's face.

"It's fine. Can we know who this person traumatizing my daughter is?" Alice's mom swiftly replied to the police chief as he flipped the file open to reveal its content of stacked documents.

"Great. Now let's journey down the rabbit hole shall we?" The police chief flashed a brief smirk as he wore a pair of reading glasses then picked up the first sheet of the documents on the pile before him. "Autumn of 1987 in this same town. A woman by the name Joan Hendrix goes missing. Now due to her constant squabbles with her husband, everyone assumed he had something to do with her disappearance and he got arrested and tried." An eerie silence enveloped the office before the police chief went on. The silence, albeit brief, was so deafening you could hear a hairpin drop to the ground. "Right before his sentencing his supposed missing wife appears out of nowhere and says she had been hypnotized by this out-of-towner."

"Wait, how long was she missing for?" Alice's mom interjected hastily as she shifted in her seat.

"A total of ninety days apparently," the police chief retorted then glanced at Alice who had a slightly confused scowl on her face. "She said she lived in some hole throughout that period and this man didn't let her climb out unsupervised." He flipped through to another document, which the police chief handed over to Alice's mom and Alice couldn't help but steal a glance which totally startled her. "The man's name was Hal. He got apprehended while trying to skip town but the state couldn't charge him then because apparently the hole he'd kept her in was not within state lines."

"Oh my god, that's him!" Alice gasped in horror as she cupped her palm over her mouth to stifle a groan of anguish that almost leapt out of her throat once her stomach churned in tight knots at the sight of Hal from the eighties. He looked exactly like he did now, except he dressed just like his supposed age in the mugshot. Wearing a dirty brown trench coat and a hat, he looked scary as he looked into the lens of the camera and Alice couldn't believe he was the same person she'd thought was the cutest in the world at a time.

"We guessed so already!" The police chief let out a sigh as he sank back in his chair, rubbing his temples at the mysterious twist the investigation was starting to take. It was clear Alice wasn't out of her mind and had definitely had an encounter with this ephemeral evil man who was passing through their town again after many decades. *What did he want and why did he choose Alice to take down such a horrendous rabbit hole. The girl had been through so much lately with losing her sister in such a manner.* The police chief clenched his jaw tightly as he resonated how quickly he'd have hunted Hal down and put a bullet in his skull if he were to go after any of his daughters or put them in a hole.

Adjusting to the edge of her seat at her daughter's sudden shocked demeanor, Alice's mom looked utterly confused and stupefied as she held the mugshot properly to Alice's view. "Honey, are you sure he's the same person? This is Hal?" she asked carefully, staring at her daughter's widened eyes.

Nodding affirmatively as the word got stuck in her throat, Alice gasped aloud. "Yes, it's him! That's Hal." She sobbed as she pulled her red face away and cupped her mouth to stifle a cry. *How stupid had she been to fall for a predator who preyed on little girls.* Her heart sank to the pit of her stomach at the realization that everything Hal told her about himself was possibly a lie. *Did he even lose his junior brother? Or was there even a brother to begin with? Why her?* These were the thoughts that plagued Alice as she tried to stifle herself from crying in front of the observant police chief and her heartbroken mother.

"How come he's still doing this? Can we get him? He needs to pay for what he's done! I mean look at her!" Alice's mom quipped rapidly at the police chief, urging him to grant her daughter some comeuppance of sorts for her trauma.

"It's alright, ma'am, we've got state troopers trawling through every nook and cranny of the town. Trust me, he's not getting far and we're gonna catch him and lock him up this time!" the police chief stated emphatically with a clenched fist on the table.

"No, you won't!" Alice, who still had her face turned towards the wall as she stifled her sobs, suddenly turned to face the police chief with puffy red eyes full of tears.

"Don't worry honey, I'm sure the police will do ev...." Alice's mom reached out to touch her daughter's shoulder but Alice shrugged her arm away.

"You guys don't get it! He's not human!" Alice retorted in a mild sob at the befuddled adults in the office who exchanged confused glances and then stared at her like she'd lost her mind.

"Hey Alice, I know you've been through a lot lately, but we need you to calm down and explain to us what you mean." The police chief adjusted his burly frame to the edge of his seat, clasping both palms before him on the table as he fixated a direct gaze at a sniffling Alice. Alice's mom also watched in silence now, heartbroken as she always was when her daughter had her emotional breakdowns.

Taking a deep breath, Alice muttered with a mild scoff, "So you'll know how to reach me...he knew I was gonna find out eventually."

"What was that honey?" Alice's mom moved closer as she heard Alice mutter something.

"The Ouija board, consulting with Jane's spirit. All of that was part of his own way of teaching me how to reach him when he disappears!" Alice replied emphatically and sank back into her chair, cupping both hands on her face and taking a deep breath before running her hands as far back as her ponytail and taking another deep breath. This was apparently so much for her to take in at once. Her mother noticed and began to pat her gently on her back.

"Easy, take slow breaths now, honey."

"This Ouija board, do you by any chance still have it in your possession?" The police chief's brown eyes narrowed at his question.

"What? No! He never let me touch it, let alone take it home. It was like his holy grail or something like that," Alice scoffed back her reply. Another tentative silence ensued in the office and just as the detective was about to say something else, there was a soft knock on the door.

"Come in!" He ushered whoever it was and a smartly dressed police officer strolled in with a piece of printed paper and handed it to the police chief. The police chief carefully scrutinized the letter as both Alice and her mom watched him with apprehensive silence.

"It would appear there was a covered up crash of an unidentified flying object twenty four hours before Hal kidnapped his first victim decades ago," the police chief announced to both mother and daughter.

Alice and her mom exchanged confused glances then back at the police chief who went on with his narration after a heavy sigh. "Apparently, an undercover manhunt was declared to find the pilot of this crashed unidentified object but no one was found. The wreckage was confiscated by the government, and I shouldn't be telling you this, but it should be somewhere out in Langley's storage unit." The police chief let out a bereaved sigh as he gently took off his glasses and wiped off a bead of sweat from his forehead. He couldn't believe what he'd just read but he knew there was a chance that this Hal might truly not be a human being after all.

"That's it..." Alice sprang up from her seat in a stunned daze. "He's an alien! It explains everything!"

"Aliens don't exist, do they?" Alice's mother was almost in tears.

"Well, I normally would say no, but with what Alice went through and what we've uncovered, I'd say I think so at this time." The police chief sat there in amazement just like Alice and her mother.

BACK HOME IN the privacy of her room, Alice's thoughts were a marauding mess as she couldn't begin to process Hal's reason for choosing her at all. *What made him want to talk to me? Hurt me? What was his end goal?* She waited until it was late at night and then reached underneath her bed to sneak out the Ouija board she'd stolen from him after the last night they had met. Unbeknownst to Hal, Alice had slid the board out of his backpack and hid it underneath a heap of dried leaves whilst they were stuck in the hole.

Taking a deep breath to steady herself, Alice spread the board just as Hal used to, and then after taking a long hard look, she decided to call Hal's name three times just like she'd done to communicate with her sister's spirit.

Just like magic, Alice watched as the board spelt out a few words as Hal's voice clearly echoed in her ears. "I'm always with you, Alice. We will be together eventually. You'll see."

Alice's heart dropped and her stomach tightened in knots as she sprang up from the floor and watched as the Ouija board clattered to the ground; scattering the words that had been formed.

THANK YOU!

Thank you for reading and I hope you enjoyed *Alice's Illusions!*

If you'd like to stay up to date on all things Maya Black, join my newsletter at https://www.subscribepage.com/p3j3r1

ABOUT THE AUTHOR

Maya Black lives in the Rocky Mountains with her husband and animals and loves being out in nature. She loves all things coffee and books!

She's a new author but has been an avid reader her whole life with stories brewing in her mind. She's finally putting pen to paper to write in a mix of genres but all will include an element of romance.

Also by Maya Black

ANTHOLOGIES

- Surviving the Unthinkable
- Genie in a Bottle
- Cracked Fairy Tales - Coming September 2024
- Twisted Fairytales- Coming September 2024
- Practical Potions - Coming October 2024
- Echoes of the Dead- Coming October 2024
- Rose of Disgrace- Coming December 2024

STANDALONES

- What Might Have Been
- Yule Spice
- Unchained Melody
- Alice's Illusions
- Wishful Witch - Coming September 2024